Lisa: *April*
Mystic Zodiac
Book 4

Brandy Walker

QUOTE:

All people think we do is dance, sing, and frolic in the water.
I wish! If that was the case I would be having a lot more fun.
~ Lisa

Welcome to the Mystic Zodiac Series.

High atop Mount Olympus, the ancient Gods and Goddesses
still reside, hidden from mortal view.
They have always been there.
WILL always be there.
Watching...
Judging...
Meddling.
They dabble in the lives of humans and lesser immortals,
known as Mystics.
For fun. Out of boredom. Simply because they can.
They thrive on watching people squirm under their thumbs.
Laugh and celebrate each other while plotting to top what
they did.

This is where our story begins...

BLURB:

A bet between Eros, the God of love & desire, and Chloe (Chlotho), the Fate of birth, leads to a year filled with matchmaking and passion.

~~~~~

For three years Lisa Cannon has been at Jack Morgan's every beck and call. As his executive personal assistant it's in the job description, except she's beginning to think she's gone above and beyond the call of duty. She hasn't had time off in so long she's pretty sure her nymph side is dying a slow death inside. After arranging for a week away, she's set to feed her nymph with every sexual fantasy that comes to mind. If they happen to all revolve around the man who keeps her tied to her desk, that's all for the better.

Jack knows he shouldn't do it but does anyway. He cancels his assistant's vacation…again. He can't stand the thought of her unleashing her nymph side on anyone but him. Over the past three years he's slowly fallen in love with the petite beauty that keeps his personal and professional life running smoothly.

When Lisa goes on vacation anyway, Jack knows there's only one thing to do. He needs to find a way into the Mystic-only club and claim the woman who has stolen his heart.

~~~~~

NOTE: Mystic Zodiac is a 12 book series. It is NOT a serial. Each book ends in a happily ever after for the main couple. However, the prologue and epilogue of each story follows the Gods that kick off the series, Eros and Chlotho (aka Chloe). At the end of the series the bet between the two will come to a conclusion.

MYSTIC ZODIAC: LISA
PROLOGUE

Chloe smoothed her soft, sky-blue chiton over her hips. Loving the feel of the fabric brushing against her skin, the way it danced around her delicate ankles. The sharp V-neck plunged low to her waist, showing her ample bosom. An enticing lure for her prey. Eros would be hers at the end of the year. She knew it down to the marrow of her bones.

Thoughts of Eros heated her blood as the memory of the previous day raced through her mind. Such excitement, mingling with humans and wearing the clothing of their realm. Eros's burning gaze as she pranced around in the tight foreign pants stretched across her backside. She glanced at the stiff canvas fabric draped on her chaise, her eyes fluttered closed at the remembered feel of him standing behind her. His thick erection pressing into her cloth-covered flesh.

It had been a stolen moment in time. She wasn't even sure he knew what he had been doing, and she dare not tell him for fear of breaking the spell.

Tearing her gaze away, she picked up a fat brush, pulling through her hair one last time. Pleased with the outcome, she tossed it on the counter before ensuring her appearance was acceptable. The last thing she wanted Eros to think was that she primped for him, yet she couldn't help but do just that. She was riding the high of stepping out of her box and enjoying the time she spent with him. It wouldn't do to have him realize she saw him as more than a delicious piece of man candy.

He unexpectedly challenged her on an intellectual level, which, in turn, aroused her beyond reason. Most men didn't dare stare into her face and talk down to her. Most men didn't resist her wants and desires. Most men were not Eros.

Chloe arrived at the Parthenon with only a few minutes to spare. Breezing through the door, she unwrapped her cloak, handing it to the servant girl waiting at the entrance. She dipped her head in respect, stroking Chloe's ego.

Chloe made her way across the room in search of the tempting as Hades man. Eros lounged in the same pillow-laden area as before. Chest gleaming, arms spread wide, muscular legs stretched out in from of him. His blond hair looked as though he'd run his hand through it time and time again. He looked freshly from bed after a night of debauchery.

Jealousy twisted in her veins and she struggled not to show it. She caught his regard as she approached, a nonchalant smile plastered on her face. Chloe immediately noticed the usual lackadaisical air that surrounded him was nowhere in sight. He grinned, yet it didn't meet his eyes. His smile was forced, and she wondered what could be wrong. Panic welled in her chest. Could he be tired of their game after only three months? Did he want to beg off? Refuse to continue now that she'd proven she was adept at matchmaking?

There was no use stressing over it. She'd find out soon enough.

"Eros," she greeted him, keeping her cool exterior pushed to the surface. Showing concern would mean showing him her vulnerability towards him.

"Chloe." He stood fluidly. "We will not have our usual time to banter today. I have been summoned by Zeus and am expected within the half hour."

"Ah. That explains the uneasy air swirling around you." Being summoned by Zeus could be good or bad. Knowing Eros, she would err on the side of bad. "Have you been cavorting with one of his consorts again?" As flippant as she tried to sound, she knew the truth. Inside she seethed at the thought. She should have known it would be too much to expect him to abstain from sex for the year of the bet. But secretly she hoped he would.

A genuine smile lit his full lips, softening the lines around his eyes. "Fear not, my sweet Chloe, I have not played where I shouldn't in quite a long time. I'm sure it is only time for my quarterly update."

She hummed noncommittally. She knew nothing of the quarterly updates other Gods and Goddesses had to endure. It was one of the perks of being a Fate. No one in the realms knew whether Zeus had control over the Fates. There was speculation running across the board as to who was really in charge. Chloe was not one to relinquish the answer. It kept others guessing and in fear of them all.

"How very…human," she murmured. "Let us get on with it then. You can be on your way to your Master and I can see if someone here catches my fancy for a few hours of entertainment."

Eros stepped within a breath away. His eyes narrowed, snapping with fire. "You will do no such thing," he said through clenched teeth. "While there is this bet, you are not to indulge your whims."

Chloe was pleased to hear his anger that she might be with someone else, yet bristled at his highhandedness. No

9

one told her what to do. Even her sisters refrained from trying. "Then neither shall you," she said, her head tipping up a notch.

They stood staring at each other, neither willing to break contact. It wasn't until the corner of his mouth curved into a sinfully wicked grin that she realized she'd made a mistake.

"Nice to know you care, my sweet. Your next couple should give you grief. She is a repressed nymph and he is human. They each have a secret—but I'll let you figure it out. You have until the end of the month, as usual."

With a swiftness she wasn't expecting, Eros clutched her to his hard body. Arm wrapped around her waist, he melded their lower halves together, grinding his erection into her soft belly. His free hand threaded into her hair, seconds before he attacked her lips like a savage getting his first taste of a woman. Lips meshed, teeth clashed. He slid his tongue into her mouth, stealing her breath. Pulling away, he bit her lower lip.

"Nine more couples Chloe and I'm yours," he said roughly. His voice thick with arousal and need.

She shivered in his hold and slid her tongue over the spot he bit, and then smiled. "The things I'm going to do to you," she whispered huskily. She stepped back and took a much-needed breath. "I'll see you next month, Eros. Don't have too good of a time at Zeus's."

Forcing one slippered foot in front of the other, Chloe glided out of the Parthenon. She wouldn't be staying like she'd told Eros. She was going home to play the encounter over and over again in her head, where no one could see her happiness.

The servant girl met her at the door, dipped and handed Chloe her cloak. Flinging it around her shoulders, she walked out the door and into the cool air. The slight breeze a blessing to her overheated body.

CHAPTER ONE

April 3rd, 8:05am

THE OFFICES OF MORGAN & POWERS
DESIGN AND ARCHITECTURE

Lisa Cannon scooted her chair close to her desk and clicked open her email. A bubble of excitement welled in her chest, threatening to burst. She was expecting the confirmation for her week away at Satyr. The exclusive club Mystics of all types went to in order to indulge in their darker side. Or in her case, let her mystic side out. It had been far too long since she'd played with her more supernatural side.

Scrolling quickly through the ridiculous amount of emails, she skipped over requests for appointments and questions for her boss. Near the bottom of the second page, she found the subject line she'd been searching for: *Satyr Thanks You*. After double clicking, instead of confirming her week of luxury and decadence, there was a terse impersonal note confirming her cancellation and inviting her to use the pre-paid amount at another date.

Oh, hell no! The phone was in her hand, and she was dialing Paul before it even became a complete thought. Fury vibrated through her. Pulling out her bottle of water, she popped the top and took a sip as the phone rang in her ear. Three rings later, Paul picked up.

"Do you know what time it is?" he grumbled on the other end. It sounded like his face was still smashed into his pillow.

"Of course I know what time it is," she snapped, unable to keep a civil tone. "I have a normal job unlike you. It's five minutes past eight."

"In the morning," his voice rose in a squeak. Lisa heard a woman admonish him, then a man's deep chuckle in the background. If Lisa knew Paul, and she did, he was back with Becks and Keith. They were an on again, off again threesome who thrived on chaos. But that drama wasn't the reason she called.

"Yes, in the morning." Her good mood had been obliterated by the email. "What the hell is this email canceling my week's stay? I've had it planned for two months now. You said everything was in place."

"What email?" Sheets rustled in the background and the bed squeaked.

"Hey, don't get up to any hanky-panky while I'm on the phone with you."

Paul snorted. "I didn't send an email."

"Well, someone did. Do I need to stress again how much I *need* this time off? I haven't let my nymph out in months. I'm pretty sure she's becoming a shriveled up shrew stuck in me."

"She's not the only one," he mumbled.

"What the hell did you just say?"

"Nothing. And, no, you don't need to tell me again. You just said hanky-panky. No nymph worth her salt would ever

12

use that phrase. Give me a second and I'll ask Becks. She worked in the office last night and I'm guessing since you didn't see it until this morning, it went out then."

Lisa grabbed her water bottle again and took a huge drink. There was mumbling on the other end of the line, but nothing she could make out. Seconds later, Paul was back. "I'm sorry, Li. It looks like your boss called last night and cancelled your plans again. Becks said he paid the fee and insisted you be able to use the pre-paid amount some other time."

The corner of Lisa's right eye started twitching the longer Paul talked. *He's done it again.* The bastard had gone behind her back and cancelled her plans. It was the fifth time so far that year. The water in her bottle started burbling uncontrollably in the container. In an automatic response, she held it off to the side, not wanting what was about to happen, to happen all over her desk. She was too fired up to stop the inevitable.

"Lisa? You still there?" Paul's voice sounded small and distant in the receiver. She knew he was speaking, but she couldn't understand the words. The buzzing in her ears slowly blocked sound out, her vision became hazy making it difficult to focus. Water spewed from the bottle shooting straight up into the air, turning into mist, hanging overhead.

It was too much. He'd gone too far this time. She'd given him two months to plan for her mini-vacation, yet he went behind her back—again. She wouldn't let him get away with it this time around. Her nerves were stretched as far as they could go, not to mention; she hadn't had sex in so long she barely remembered what it felt like.

The door leading into her office opened. In walked the dynamic duo that made up Morgan & Powers Design and Architecture: Jack Morgan and Griffin Powers.

"I have to go," she said to Paul, not bothering to wait for a reply. She dropped the receiver into the cradle unnoticed, glaring at the men. Granted, it wasn't Griffin's fault her morning had gone to shit, but the fact that his best friend was the devil made him guilty by association.

Griffin, the poor clueless soul, halted next to her desk, a charming smile plastered on his face. "You're on vacation next week, right? You must be excited to get away from Jack's needy ass for a while." He chuckled and tipped his head toward his business partner.

Lisa made the mistake of glancing at her boss; a knowing smirk curved his sexy lips. Her control snapped seeing him gloat and soft mist suddenly rained down on Griffin's head.

Griffin jumped back in surprise as his expensive suit soaked up most of the water. He looked around confused, and then his eyes landed on Lisa, who was still holding the now empty bottle away from her. "Um, hey Lisa. Is there," he looked up at the ceiling, frowned, and then focused back on her, "a problem with the sprinkler system?"

"No," she gritted out. She breathed slowly, attempting to rein in her anger. It never failed. If water was nearby when she lost it—it went everywhere. She didn't know if it was a perk or a curse of her nymph side. At the moment, she wished it had been Jack standing in Griffin's place. He was the one who deserved something bad happening to him.

Griffin's eyes widened briefly before he turned his attention to Jack. "What did you do?" He asked, disappointment evident in his voice. Griffin was the nice guy of her two bosses. The one who went the extra mile to help someone out. The one who gave a person the benefit of the doubt. And apparently the one who knew not to fuck with a desperate woman's vacation plans.

Jack held up his hands. "Nothing," he said innocently, "I swear." He grinned like the devil he was. She didn't believe him and she doubted Griffin did either.

Griffin snorted. "Yes you did. I may not understand her mystic powers or much about that world, but I know she

14

only does that when she's pissed—at you. How I ended up on the receiving end is beyond me."

Lisa stood slowly. Breathing in deep, she dropped the bottle in the trash, and then gathered napkins to blot the water on Griffin's suit jacket. "I'm sorry about that, Mr. Powers. It won't happen again." Invading his space, she dabbed at his chest.

"I've told you to call me Griff."

"And I've told you that I can't call my boss by his first name."

"Then at least do it to piss him off," he whispered none too quietly. She knew he did it to get a reaction from his partner. They both liked to pull each other's chains. She wouldn't be taking part in it though.

Lisa shook her head and continued soaking up the water. It wasn't as bad as she previously thought. The heat in the room must have evaporated some of it.

Out of the corner of her eye, she noticed Griffin's eyebrows shoot into his hairline as she skimmed her hand down his muscular chest toward his trim waist. *All in the name of collecting water droplets*, she mused.

Stepping back, she looked him over, making sure she'd gotten as much as she could. The jacket was good, but his hair—stepping closer than she'd been before because of her height, she reached up to brush her fingers through his thick black locks when he captured her wrists with his big hands. Her startled gaze landed on his amused one. Griffin looked beyond her to Jack, who had yet to say another word.

"I've got it," Griffin said.

It was then she noticed exactly how close she was to him. How intimate the two of them looked. She cleared her throat and stepped back. "Sorry, again." Her cheeks flushed hot and she was grateful for her darker complexion. Better they not see how flustered she really was.

Jack and Griffin were both sexy as hell, but she was their employee. Nothing would ever come of her lusting over the men, especially Jack.

They towered over her five-foot two, petite frame. Even when she overcompensated with heels, which she did every day; it didn't make much of a difference. When she stood next to them, she felt like a child and not the highly independent twenty-eight year old woman she was.

Looking at them, you wouldn't know they were architects unless you knew them on a professional or personal level. Broad shoulders. Tapered waists. Muscular arms and thighs evident behind the soft fabric of their suits. They were a visual feast she'd eaten up more than once. One more than the other. *Damn devil.*

Lisa knew for a fact they both worked out. She'd been keeping up on Jack's gym membership for the last three years since becoming his executive personal assistant, and the men didn't do many things without the other. There were times when she wondered if they did *everything* together. The nymph in her begged her to find out. Luckily, she'd been able to hold the randy nymph back, which brought her back to her current problem.

"What did he do this time?" Griffin asked, raking his fingers through his midnight black hair.

"Canceled my vacation plans again."

Griffin's navy blue eyes widened in surprise. "Again?"

"Don't act as if you don't know. You two can't go a day without gossiping around the water cooler." She moved back to her seat, tossing the wet napkins into the trash.

"We don't have a water cooler," Griff quipped cheekily.

Lisa wanted to smack him for that comment. Instead,

she straightened files and made sure nothing else had gotten wet. "You know what I mean. And, yes, again. I have so much unused vacation time I could quit today and still get paid for a year."

"Not gonna happen," Jack finally voiced, steel threading through the words. Striding across the room, she couldn't tear her eyes away from him. He moved with power and grace. Like a predator hunting his prey. When she first met him, she thought he was a Mystic, a supernatural being like her. Not quite a God or Goddess, but so much more than a human. Later, she found her initial impression was wrong. As she spent more time with him, it was clear he didn't set off any of her mystic *woo-woo* radar triggers. She'd been unusually disappointed.

Jack edged closer to her desk. Her breath caught when he planted his powerful body in front of her. His dark gray suit was tailored to fit him in the best possible way. Highlighting every sharp angle and hard ridge. The nymph tried to push to the forefront, and Lisa struggled to contain her. Her gaze drifted lower to his crotch before she could stop herself.

She squeezed her eyes shut. This was exactly why she needed her vacation.

Jack, that bastard, had her body reacting quicker with each passing day. The man could breathe and she was ready to jump his damn bones. Her fingers itched to run through his dark-brown shaggy hair. His forest-green eyes with flecks of melted chocolate hypnotized her into a pliant, willing woman when their gazes clashed. His full lips, straight white teeth, and chiseled jaw made him a beautiful, rugged man she wanted to throw on the ground and take advantage of.

Lately, her attraction to him was posing a damn big problem. Locking down her body's reaction was making the situation impossible. She worked for him, which was why she set up the week at Satyr. She planned on working out her *Jack induced* fantasies on a man who reminded her of him. A man who didn't mind if she screamed someone else's name as she shattered around him.

Lisa folded her hands in front of her, gathering her composure. "You really have no say in what I do, which brings us back to you cancelling my plans. Mr. Morgan, you've had two months to get accustomed to the idea of me taking time off. I had hoped, with the advance notice, you'd have an easier time accepting this break."

"Now isn't a good time, Lisa," he commented as if she didn't know his schedule. She made the damn thing, and knew there wasn't anything pressing going on. The chance of something coming up between quitting time the previous night and start of business this morning was slim to none.

"What is so important you needed me here? The Perkins presentation isn't due for three more weeks. You don't have any travel coming up until after I get back. There are no projects or clients that need researched. There isn't anything going on that Mr. Power's assistant, Janet, can't handle while I'm out."

"What about the supplies? It's the beginning of the month, and I know that's when you do whatever you do."

"The office supplies have been ordered and will be stocked and distributed as per the memo I sent to Phillips."

Jack clenched his jaw, nostrils flaring. He didn't like what she'd laid out in front of him, but too damn bad. She needed the time away from him to sate her nymph. It had been too long and, even though she'd learned to deal with her wild side locked up for long periods of time, the situation she was currently in bordered on the ridiculous.

"It doesn't matter now," he proclaimed. "You'll have to figure out another time to take vacation. I doubt you'll be able to get your reservations back anyway." He glanced at his watch. "I believe the Carter phone conference is starting soon. We'll take the usual."

Jack turned away, as if he hadn't just ruined her life,

18

heading to his office without a backwards glance. Griffin lagged behind, sympathy pouring off him. "If you ever want to work with someone who isn't an ass, I'd be happy to kick Janet to the curb."

Lisa chuckled. She knew he wasn't entirely serious. It was his way of smoothing things over when his friend was a dick. "I might take you up on that offer. Will you give me time off?"

Griffin grinned. "Of course. Whenever you want—as long as I get to come."

"That would defeat the purpose. Does Janet know you keep offering me her job?"

"Yep, she said the sooner you accept, the better. She's sick of my ass, and is ready to follow in Claire's footsteps. Janet wants to take her young stud on a trip around the world. And I don't know if she means actual travel or something I really don't want to know about." He saluted her quickly and joined Jack, leaving her laughing at his parting comment.

CHAPTER TWO

Jack paced his office waiting for Griffin to join him. What could possibly be taking the man so long? There was nothing the two of them needed to talk about, unless Griff was attempting to steal Lisa away again. *Bastard*!

Lisa's bright laughter stopped him in his tracks. He could hear the amusement in the sound. Griff had gotten the woman to lighten up and probably smile at his stupid face. Jack's hands curled into fists, knuckles popping the tighter they got. Irrational, possessive feelings bombarded him; setting off a deep need to kick his best friend's ass. The only problem with that was the fact Lisa was his assistant not his girlfriend. Damned if he didn't want her to be though. To be truthful, he wanted more than boyfriend status. He wanted the right to own every moment of every day.

Rolling his shoulders, Jack took a deep breath. Nothing was going on between his friend and his assistant. Griff wasn't interested in Lisa, at least not anything beyond finding her an attractive woman. Ever since *the incident*, Griff had shied away from romantic entanglements. That was the only reason Jack could force himself to relax.

Moving behind his desk, he took a seat in his high-backed leather chair. Waking up his computer, he found it ready for the phone conference. The specs of the house they were designing were on one screen, the photos of the land on the other. It had been Lisa's idea to set up the dual monitors. Jack figured it would be a pain in the ass to have to jump between them while trying to work. She'd won the battle of him giving it a try, now he couldn't imagine working without them. It was one more thing he loved about her. She didn't roll over and let him do what he wanted.

Worry flickered through his chest as he thought about his parting shot. She could take his words as a challenge and find a way to take her vacation after all. He could only hope what he'd said was true. That she wouldn't be able to reclaim her reservations. He'd heard it was tough to get into Satyr. He probably should have thought through his hasty last minute decision.

It didn't help he hadn't had a leg to stand on when she asked what was so important he needed her at work. He should have had a believable reason ready. He sucked at coming up with things on the fly. That was Griff's area of expertise.

Lisa was beyond efficient at her job, and the best assistant he'd ever had. He didn't want to lose her, but he couldn't stop himself from lusting after her. She tied him in knots without even knowing it: independent nature and keen intellect, along with form fitting suits that showed every subtle dip and curve. The fuck-me heels she wore everyday; showing off her slim legs and perfect calves. It all made for a stunning package and her beautiful face topped it all off. Her deep red lips and deep brown eyes set off her darker complexion. It was a wonder he made it through each day without taking her on the first flat surface he could find.

It had been on the tip of his tongue to tell her he wasn't going to allow her to let her nymph out on anyone but him. He saw glimpses of the saucy, free-spirited woman who lurked beneath the surface. The heated looks she shot his way when she didn't think he was looking. The seductress who could sweet-talk even the grumpiest of clients into agreeing with their plans.

She wasn't overly flirtatious with men or women. She didn't promise them one thing then deliver another. She charmed them. Seduced them. Pulled them into her way of thinking while keeping it professional. She was a force to be reckoned with and, damn, that turned him on.

Griff finally opened the door and stepped inside. He shut it behind him before taking a seat across from Jack. As per usual, he slumped down in the chair, feet stretched out in front of him. "You need to quit, Jack. That woman is going to blow and soon. Hell, she's already sprayed water all over the place."

Jack grimaced. It had been a dick move, but he couldn't stand the thought of her playing in that pleasure palace without him. "At least it evaporated — mostly."

"What did she have planned?"

Jack snorted. "A week at Satyr." It was one of the most exclusive clubs in the city. It catered to a certain clientele, and he'd yet to gain acceptance. There was an extensive background and genealogy search, and he'd been told it could take six months to a year for it to be complete. He was sick of waiting and beginning to wonder if there was another way in.

Breath whooshed loudly out of Griff. "Damn. That had to cost a pretty penny."

"It did," more than Jack had expected. "It isn't like she's out the money. I explained to the woman I talked to that something had come up unexpectedly. I paid the cancellation fee and ensured Lisa could use the pre-paid amount another time."

"I'm sure she'll appreciate that later. Right now — I'm

pretty sure she's thinking of ways to maim you. And you're seriously going to allow her to go to Satyr?"

"Only if she's with me. The thought of her going there and dallying with some idiot makes me want to commit murder."

"That may not be the best way to win her over."

Jack shrugged. "I can't take it anymore. I need to find a way to get what I want."

"By anymore you mean…" Griff trailed off, waiting for Jack to fill in the rest.

"I mean I want to lock her in my office and fuck her senseless. Erase every man she's ever been with from her mind. Then I want to take her home and keep her there until she promises to be mine forever. Even then, I'm not sure I'd let her go."

"You've got it pretty bad."

"No shit," Jack muttered.

The room fell silent. A hesitant knock sounded at the door. A couple seconds passed before Lisa turned the knob and came in, balancing a tray with two cups, sugar, creamer and two pastries on one hand. She set it down on his desk and walked around to stand next to Jack. Lisa leaned across him, brushing her nubile body against him, then brought a new window up on one of the monitors. Backtracking and leaving him on edge, she left without a word, the door shutting silently behind her.

Jack took a ragged breath. The crisp scent of a dewy morning rain filled his lungs. His erection tented the fabric of his pants easily, throbbing with the need to feel the tight clamp of her pussy. If she broke the ironclad hold she had on her nymph and gave the slightest hint she was ready for more, he could have his cock out and in her in seconds.

"You're going to have to fire her," Griff said, pulling him from the fantasy of Lisa wrapped around him.

Jack's eyebrow shot up, as he came back down to planet earth. "Like hell."

Griff shook his head. "Take it from me, don't mess with the hired help. It'll only get you in trouble."

Ah, yes. The incident. Griff knew all too well what happened when a person fooled around with the help. When Janet, his regular assistant, ended up in the hospital with pneumonia, they'd pulled a secretary from the drafting department. The temp pursued Griff like he was the last man on earth, and they had a brief affair. When Janet came back, the woman tried to force Griff to fire Janet so she could keep the job, along with her status as Griff's lover. In the end, they cut the woman a very nice severance check and gave her a paid holiday.

"Lisa isn't like Felicity and you know it."

"Yeah, but I don't know for sure," Griff grumbled. "I don't want you to go through what I did, Jack."

"I won't. You know Lisa, man. Her work ethic is better than ours, and we're pretty fucking dedicated. She's never asked for anything in all of the years she's been here, and she's never used her gorgeous assets to get ahead. She'd never pull a stunt like Felicity. It isn't in her."

"I don't know." Griff shook his head ruefully. It killed Jack to see him like that. The most giving, laidback guy he knew was an uptight gun-shy man. After a second, his face screwed up into a look of resignation. "You better make sure that's true before you go down this road. I don't want to see you get hurt, and I'd hate for the company to lose her."

"Well, I don't need to figure it out right now. Her vacation is off for the moment, and we have a client about to call."

CHAPTER THREE

Lisa logged onto the temp agency she used when she needed extra hands in the company. She hadn't planned on bringing anyone in since Janet offered to help out, but Jack deserved to have things shaken up. He needed to see she was serious about having time away. And she wasn't going to allow for the comfort of the familiar. It was time to look for a stand-in so she could have some time off. Jack was finished screwing her over.

As soon as she shut the door behind her after delivering the guys their morning breakfast, her mind began to whirl. There was no way she'd be able to stand another month, let alone another week, of being around him without jumping his bones. He was off limits, and had been from day one when she'd joined the company.

Opening his office door, she'd immediately felt his gaze land on her, tracking her progress into the room. Her nipples peaked beneath her blazer. A shiver raced down her petite frame. The nymph in her clawed to break free as she'd stood there next to him breathing in his musky, woodsy scent.

It tugged at her. Taunted her. Turned her on like nobody's business.

The scent reminded her of the times she used to frolic in the woods behind her home with her sisters. The nights spent splashing in the lake under the moonlight. The freedom. The pure pleasure. The decadence and carnality.

No. She needed to get away from him if she stood any chance of working with him any longer. She needed to escape the need pounding down on her each minute he was near. She didn't actually know if time at Satyr would help, but it was the only thing she could think of. In the past, it'd taken off the edge. She was afraid she'd gone too long without going nymph for the break to have any effect.

Lisa typed in the requirements her replacement would need. Not thinking twice when she specified a more mature assistant. No need to tempt him with a young, willing substitute.

Oh, how greedy you are, the inner voice in her head taunted. She may not be able to have him, but she sure as hell wouldn't watch some other woman get him.

She got down to the area for the dates needed. Nibbling on her lip, she wasn't quite sure what she should select. Two months notice certainly didn't work with the man. Thinking back on all of the other times, she realized giving him any notice at all tended to backfire. She would have to spring it on him and deal with the consequences later.

Grabbing up the receiver of her phone, she dialed Paul again. He picked up immediately.

"Hey, Li. I figured I'd be hearing from you again." He sounded a lot more awake than he had earlier. He'd probably gotten laid and had coffee in the time since she'd hung up on him.

"Can you re-do my reservation? Everything the same as before." She pulled up Jack's schedule as she spoke in case

Paul couldn't come through for her.

Papers crinkled and she heard the distinct sound of him tapping on his keyboard. At least she'd get a quick answer and not have to wait for a callback later. "Sorry, babe. Once you cancelled, Cosmo went to the next on the list. The automatic system took care of it. He's in high demand, ya know."

"That's fine. I can deal with that. Is my room at least still available?"

"Yep. I haven't gotten around to checking it out to anyone."

"Well, don't. I'll take it from the sixth to the tenth. That will give me the weekend to make sure everything is good at work and a weekend to recover from my time there."

"What about your boss? Face it sweets, he isn't going to like you coming here, and I won't be able to retain the money you already spent if you cancel again."

"It wasn't my fault," she huffed. "And fuck him!"

"Maybe you should," Paul snickered. It wasn't the first time he'd suggested the naughty idea. He'd even gone as far as planning out how she should seduce him. It involved a tight short skirt, killer heels, and her trapping him in his office chair as she gave him a lap dance. "You two need to get it out of your systems. You're hot under the hood for that man. And you know the only reason he keeps doing this is because he wants to be your boy toy when you get down and nasty."

"He doesn't even know what getting nasty with me entails," she snorted. There was truth behind the term *nymphomaniac* when it was applied to her. While all nymphs enjoyed a good roll in the hay, her locking her nymph up to work in the business world meant when she was let out, she indulged like a drug addict with a fresh supply easily on hand. "And he won't. He's my boss and that's all he'll ever be. You know my rules…and the company policy."

"Oh please! He'd break that policy in a heartbeat if it meant he could get between your toned thighs."

"I'm not giving him the chance. Reserve next week for me. I think I'm going to let the nymph take complete control. Maybe check out some of the open playrooms. I need to get Jack out of my system."

"He hasn't even gotten *in* you yet." Paul mumbled.

"Just do it, please, Paul. I'm desperate here."

Paul's heavy sighed reached her through the phone. "Whatever you say, babe. I've got you down." Thank god he relented without giving her more flack.

The internal office buzzer sounded from the speaker. She was being summoned. "I've got to go. Love ya, Paul. You're the best."

Paul hung up after saying goodbye. Lisa picked up her notepad and pencil, diminished the screen for the temp agency, and took a couple of deep breaths. She needed to slip the cool, controlled mask onto her face before joining her bosses.

Plastering a smile on, she breezed through the door. The look of concern on Jack's face and the knowledge that he wasn't having the last laugh erased her foul mood. Vacation was back on and there wasn't a damn thing Jack Morgan could do to stop it from happening this time.

CHAPTER FOUR

April 6th, 8:00am

THE OFFICES OF MORGAN & POWERS DESIGN AND
ARCHITECTURE

Jack rode the elevator up to his floor, hands shoved in his pockets, whistling a soft tune. A cool sense of calm flowed through him as floor after floor whizzed by until he stopped on eight. The door slid open and Lisa's soft scent drifted over him. He could pick it out anywhere, even with the smallest amount present. *She must be in already*, he mused, stepping into the corridor.

His day tended to begin and end with her on his mind. Some would say it was the nature of their relationship. The endless hours working together; sometimes in intimate settings. Dinners together with clients. Black tie charity auctions. Closed up in his condo late into the night.

It was more than moments in time that kept her on his mind. She'd taken up residence before he'd gotten to know her, starting the day she filled in for his previous assistant Claire. At first, it was purely physical. Noticing her petite, lithe body the second she'd walked through his office door to introduce herself. A wave of protective instincts washed over him as she slid her small hand into his. She was tiny compared to him, even when she wore her sexy as hell heels.

Part of him wanted to fire her right then and there. But he was fairly sure asking her out on a date right after firing her wouldn't work out in his favor. He'd planned on finding her after her stint as a fill-in at his office, but his secretary abruptly quit in order to join the younger man she'd been dating on a world traveling adventure. Lisa already knew the ins and outs of his schedule, so like the dumb ass he was; he offered her the job as his new permanent assistant.

Three years later and he couldn't imagine his life without her. She'd become the one person besides Griffin he could count on. She was the only other person to care about him as a man and not just as the wealthy head of a multi-million dollar company.

His love, for as long as he could remember, had been architecture until the last couple of years. When Lisa entered his life, he realized he'd found something—someone—that filled a corner of his heart he hadn't known was empty. He wasn't about to let her go, not now…not ever. He knew in his heart they could make a relationship work. If she wanted to stay his assistant, he was all for it. If she wanted to quit and be a stay at home wife and eventual mother, he was all for that as well. He would do whatever she wanted as long as she vowed to be by his side forever.

And to make up for his dick move of cancelling her plans, he gave her the weekend off. He didn't even call her. It was the magnanimous thing to do. He also hoped it would give her time to get over being pissed at him. Surely, she wouldn't hold a grudge against him after a weekend away.

Pushing through Lisa's office door, he looked to her desk, expecting her shining face to greet him. Instead of seeing her short dark hair, creamy cocoa skin, and a smile that set him on fire; there sat a graying, older woman with crinkles around the corners of her mouth. She smiled gently from Lisa's chair.

"Good morning, Mr. Morgan." She stood and held out

a stack of mail. "Ms. Cannon briefed me on this week's schedule. Nothing too pressing, so I'm sure I'll have no problem handling it."

Jack took the mail from the woman, his mind whirling. What the hell was going on? Was Lisa sick? Did she get into an accident? Panic welled in his chest threatening to steal his breath. She didn't call him to tell him anything was wrong, so why was there a stranger occupying her desk? Heading into his office, the woman followed, oblivious to his tumultuous thoughts.

"I have your computer booted and ready for your morning meeting. I'm assuming Mr. Powers will be joining you soon. I'll bring the coffee and pastries in once he arrives. I understand they are to be heated enough to make them melt in your mouth. "

Jack walked around his desk and sat. "Excuse me, miss..." he trailed off.

She blushed, her pale cheeks turning pink. "Oh, I'm so sorry, Mr. Morgan. I'm Mrs. French. I'm from the temp agency. I'll be filling in for Ms. Cannon while she's out this week. I assure you, I'm well qualified for the position. On Saturday, Ms. Cannon spent an hour going over my qualifications and references and another two hours showing me the ropes. If you'd like, I can bring my references to you."

Jack forced the charming smile that had women telling him their every secret and fantasy onto his face. "I have no doubt you're qualified. Ms. Cannon is excellent at her job. Were you given a reason why you needed to fill in for Li... her?"

"Of course, Mr. Morgan," she said without batting an eye. She also didn't give him the reason.

He stared expectantly and waited for her to crack, but the tight-lipped older woman wasn't forthcoming. Griff walked into the room, brows dipping down when he glanced at Mrs. French standing in front of the desk. "Hey

31

Jack, what's going on? I didn't see Lisa at her desk. Is she running late?"

Jack gave him a *no shit* look and tilted his head toward Mrs. French. "Ms. Cannon is out for the week. Mrs. French will be filling in for her while she's gone."

Griff's unsettled gaze drifted to the woman in question. "Is Lisa, uh, I mean Ms. Cannon alright?"

"Why wouldn't she be?" Mrs. French asked in confusion. Her forehead pinched and lips puckered.

Griff shrugged. "I didn't know she was going to be gone this week. That's all."

"I wouldn't expect she'd tell you, Mr. Powers. She *is* Mr. Morgan's assistant and not yours," she admonished. The starch in her voice putting them both in their places.

Like the recalcitrant boy Griff used to be, he dropped his head. "Yes ma'am," he mumbled.

Jack chuckled and received a hardened glare from her. He smothered his laughter behind a cough. "Yes, well, we'll take our coffee and pastries, please."

She gave a sharp nod. "Very good. The documents for your morning meeting are in the folder on your desk. The sketches have been brought up on your computer." She turned stiffly and strode out of the room with her head held in an imperious manner.

Griff swung the door shut behind her and plopped into a chair. "What the hell? Did you know about this?"

"If I did, do you think I'd still be sitting here?" The vein in Jack's temple throbbed. He felt a headache forming. How could Lisa do this to him? He hadn't authorized the time off. Shit, he'd thought he'd nipped this whole vacation thing in the bud.

"Where do you think she is?"

"If I had to guess…Satyr," Jack growled. The throbbing in his head grew stronger.

"You think she would go without telling you? You know what, never mind. I told you to quit messing with her plans. You're getting exactly what you deserve."

Mrs. French walked in unannounced carrying the breakfast tray, and they waited for her to leave, shutting the door behind her.

"Well, she's going get her own little surprise. I'm done waiting for that background check. I'm going to Satyr and getting my woman."

Griff tossed his head back and laughed. Jack didn't find the situation the least bit funny. The day of reckoning was coming for Miss Lisa Cannon, and she damn well better be prepared for the punishment she was about to get. He could imagine it now, tossing her over his lap and paddling her ass for defying him. She would beg for forgiveness, then, and only then, would he show her precisely why they were meant to be together.

33

CHAPTER FIVE

April 6th, 11:00am

SATYR – THE RETREAT

"This is heaven," Lisa breathed out slowly. And exactly what she needed.

After checking into her suite an hour ago, Lisa had unpacked her suitcase, ordered lunch to be delivered at noon, and was relishing in the first of many luxuries to be had over the upcoming week.

She leaned back in the massive tub, disturbing the bubbles around her. Lavender floated in the air, soothing her ragged nerves. She sighed, her eyes fluttering closed when the jets turned on and tension flowed from her body.

"Holy crap that's wonderful." She couldn't think of the last time she'd been able to take a bath. To play in the rejuvenating waters that were a large part of who she was. No wonder her nymph side got cranky. They'd been apart from an elemental part of their soul for much too long.

Quick showers were her only connection as of late. Fast, unfulfilling ones where she scrubbed the grime of the day off before falling into bed. For the last couple of months, her life revolved more and more around Jack and his needs, while sacrificing the needs of her nymph.

"Not any more." Taking a deep breath, Lisa scooped up water in each of her hands. Eyes closed and head tilted back; she called to the spirit ruling her soul.

I invoke you, Mother of the naiad, who rules over the power of
water
Goddess of energy, wisdom, passion and desire
Mistress of lake, river, spring or fountain
Please come to me, flow through my veins
Allow me to be my destiny.

A warm breezed swirled around her, lifting her hair and caressing her face. The Goddess answered her call. The water jumped in her hands. Churning...twisting into a funnel as she brought them together. Thrusting her offering forward, the funnel broke, the water spewing away from her and back into the tub.

The breeze disappeared and when she opened her eyes again, it was with clear vision and lighter heart.

A knock sounded on her outer door, a muffled *room service* making its way through the thick barrier. Climbing out of the tub, she drained it and wrapped a warm towel around her. She had no intention of putting clothes on at the moment. The urge to walk around naked was too much to resist.

Pulling the door open, she was greeted by a tall, delicious-looking man. His midnight black skin gleamed under the lights in the hallway. He tipped his head down, a slight nod to submission. "Your meal ma'am."

Waving him in, Lisa trailed behind him, more than happy to check the enticing view. The nymph in her slowly awoke from her water-induced high, appreciating the man before her. His tight leather pants hugged his firm ass like a second skin. She wanted to smack it and hear the sound crack through the room. Her gaze traveled up over his thick, bare muscular back. She noticed scars crossing down over his broad shoulders onto the upper part. Her fingers itched to trace the marks. To find out if they were as smooth and taut as they appeared. To test how much feeling he had in the slightly raised blemishes.

He placed the tray on her table near the window. As he uncovered the dishes she'd ordered, she grabbed some money from her purse. It wasn't necessary to tip in the traditional manner. Satyr allowed for alternate forms of payment to the Mystics who worked there. But being in the business world for so long and dealing with more humans than her kind, it was habit.

The man stepped to the side as she approached the table. A grin curved the corner of his mouth. A sexy smirk telling her he knew she'd checked him out. He'd probably planned it that way. "I'm happy to feed you ma'am, if that is your wish." His deep baritone slid sensuously from his full lips.

Lisa couldn't say what made her hesitate, but she did. She paused; mouth open ready to say yes, yet nothing came out.

The man invited her attention. Lust was stamped on his face as he perused every inch of her. She felt the heat of his stare through her towel. The offer to feed her, which she knew would result in him sitting at her feet submissively, his hard packed muscles begging to be touched and fondled — grazed and nipped, should have been tempting her beyond reason.

She did a systems check of her body. There was no racing heart. No slither of arousal through her veins. No excitement or anticipation of what would follow. There wasn't a fiber in her being aching to do more than have a cursory look or to enjoy the beauty in his body as a visual feast. The nymph didn't clamor to tear his clothes from his body.

She smiled softly and pressed the money in his hand.

There was no reaction from her nymph. No spark to do more. "Thank you. Maybe some other time," she said gently and escorted him to the door.

He stopped outside the threshold. "When you're ready, call guest services and request me. My name is Kyron. I would be more than happy to bring you pleasure." He ran a hot look over her before picking up her hand and placing a kiss on the inside of her wrist. His tongue flicked over her pulse, and she thought she should change her mind. She'd bet he could do wicked things with his tongue. Things she hadn't experienced in far too long.

But when she imagined laying claim to hulking Kyron, he morphed into the last person she should have lustful thoughts about...Jack. Even on vacation the man refused to vacate her mind.

CHAPTER SIX

April 6th, 1:00pm

THE OFFICES OF MORGAN & POWERS DESIGN AND ARCHITECTURE

"What do you mean the background check isn't complete?" Jack barked into the phone. The first chance he had he'd called Satyr. First, to the registration desk to find out if Lisa was a registered guest. When they wouldn't tell him, he hung up and called the membership liaison to check on his application.

"Like I said, Mr. Morgan," the nasally man on the other end of the line grated out. "There are a couple more relations we need to investigate before we can make a decision one way or the other."

"You've had the application for almost a year. What is it in my background you can't find?"

"At the present time, Mr. Morgan, a Mystic. If you knew for sure you had Mystic blood running through your veins and what kind, the investigation would have been over months ago. As it is, we've only found one loose connection to an angel dating back four generations, but we cannot confirm the verification. We've been unable to contact the

Mystic in question. Our researchers are following proper procedure to ensure the validity of the relation. We'll let you know when our findings are complete."

The man hung up before Jack could say anything more. It was probably a good thing he had too.

"Fuck," Jack roared, slamming the phone down. What the hell was he supposed to do now? He couldn't very well head to the club and demand entrance. No one did that. The security was tight, and unless you were a member, you weren't getting in. Not even guests were allowed unless they had easily proved Mystic abilities, or had received a special invitation. He didn't think he knew anyone who could get him one of those.

"What's up, Jack?" Griff asked sauntering into his office, then taking a seat across from him.

"I just got off the phone with Satyr. They won't tell me if Lisa is registered as a guest, and my application hasn't been processed yet. I'm not Mystic enough at this point to be allowed entrance. I have to wait until their research is complete."

"Even then you still might not be allowed in. If they don't find anything in the background, they'll toss your application on the burn pile. No one gets in unless they're approved."

"Fuck," Jack grunted again. He leaned back in his chair and pushed his fingers through his hair. Frustration ate at him the longer he was away from Lisa. She could be having the time of her life with some random guy at that very moment.

"Here," Griff said grabbing Jack's attention. He looked to see his friend holding out a pale blue business card.

"What is it?" He asked, reaching across the desk.

Griff's mouth pulled down into a frown, his grip

tightening on the paper. "Mrs. French gave it to me as I was coming in. She said you might want to call the number listed if your plan didn't work out. Whoever this is has some pull and might be able to get you in."

"Why do you seem reluctant to give it to me?"

"I don't want you to make a mistake. I like Lisa. In fact, I think she's great."

"But…"

"But I don't want you to get your hopes up about having a lasting relationship with the woman. She's a nymph. They're known for playing with people's emotions. They're ambivalent, fickle, and salacious. She may only be interested in having a quick affair. Last I heard, most nymphs don't settle down."

Jack felt the burn of anger fire in his chest. "Where the fuck did you get that information?" He knew Griff was trying to be a friend, look out for him. The man forgot one very important thing. "She's not like most nymphs."

"I know. I did a little research online. I was concerned."

"Don't be. I'm sure how I feel about her, and I think she feels the same. Lisa has worked her ass off for the last ten years to prove she isn't anything like the stereotype."

"How do you know?"

"I've talked to her. Hell, we spend more time together than most married couples. I feel like I know her inside and out. She grew up in a big family with a bunch of sisters and a couple of brothers. They all frolicked and played, enticing men and women to abandon their responsibilities. Lisa did too, at least for a little while. She tired of being interchangeable. She also tired of no one seeing her for who she was, and only seeing that typecast character of a nymph. She wanted more and she went out and got it. I admire her tenacity."

"Oh," Griff said softly. "I didn't know."

"Now you do, so can I please have the card? I'm serious about her Griff, and I'm past the point of caring what will happen. I need to tell her before I go insane. I can figure out what to do next depending on her reaction. But I swear, deep down I know it'll be good."

Griff let go of the card they'd held between them. Jack quickly scanned it to see what it was all about. In bold black lettering it read:

Your Fate is in your hand
Chloe: 699-3283

Jack flipped the card over. There wasn't anything on the back. "You say Mrs. French gave this to you? Where'd she get it?"

Griff shrugged and slouched in the chair. "I was walking by when she stopped me and handed me the card."

Jack hit the speaker button on his phone. "Mrs. French, could I see you a moment?"

There was no reply, so he tried again. "Mrs. French?" An uneasy feeling started in the pit of Jack's stomach. Before he could stand and check on his temporary assistant, Griff got to his feet.

"I'll check on her. You give that number a call. I just want you to be happy." He left, closing the door behind him.

Jack tapped the card on the desk, stalling. Too many thoughts bombarded him. The card could be a joke. The number on it a scam of some sort. The worst that could happen was someone would be sitting back laughing at him for falling for a prank. But how did Mrs. French know he was trying to get into Satyr? He hadn't said anything to her, and he didn't think Griff had either. They kept their conversations about the place confined to the office.

But what if the person on the other end of the line could get him in? What if Chloe knew the answer to what he most wanted?

There was only one way to find out.

Picking up the receiver, he punched the speaker button and dialed the number. A woman with a husky voice answered after the first ring.

"It took you long enough," she said, irritation lacing her voice.

"Um, my assistant, well temporary assistant, wait — who is this, and do you know who I am?"

"You dialed me Jack, so you know who I am."

"You're Chloe?" How the hell did she know who he was? *Caller ID maybe.*

"Yes and to answer your question, I have my ways and, no, it isn't caller ID. Whatever that is. Let's get down to business. I have things to do today that do not involve talking on this...thing."

"My temporary assistant gave me your card and said you might be able to help me get into Satyr."

"My dear human, she did no such thing. She gave the card to your cute friend and told *him* I could help you."

"Same difference."

She sighed heavily. "The one you seek is at Satyr. She is checked in for the week. Your Mystic blood is too weak to gain you entrance. The research team won't be able to verify your loose connection."

"Then you can't help me," he interrupted, aggravated by the conversation already.

"You humans have no patience," she bit out.

The line went dead and Jack was left holding the receiver in his hand. He was staring dumbly at it when a warm swirl of air spread through his office. It flowed around him, licking at the exposed skin of his arms, up his neck, and fluttering over his face. His vision turned fuzzy, and he blinked rapidly to clear it, but to no avail. When it finally did clear, there was a tall, statuesque woman and a mountain of a man standing before him.

Jack jumped from his seat, stumbling back in surprise. He dropped the phone and nearly tripped over his chair. "What the *fuck*?"

"Watch your tongue," the man snarled, his dark eyebrow lifting in warning.

"Who the hell are you two?"

The woman laughed. "Not from Hell, Jack. Not even close." She turned to the man next to her. "Is he one of yours, Gabriel?"

The man, Gabriel, focused dark eyes on him, giving Jack the feeling he was being judged. He stood rooted in place, the weight of the scrutiny keeping him from moving. After moments of intense visual inspection, Gabriel came around the desk and grabbed Jack's right arm. He shoved the shirtsleeve up further, revealing the spear-shaped birthmark on the inside of his bicep.

Gabriel nodded sharply and let go, stepping back to Chloe's side. "He is. He bears my mark."

"So reckless, Gabriel. I wonder what the others would say," she chided.

Gabriel's deep chuckle filled the room. "Nothing. I have done nothing they haven't. How do you think we keep our ranks strong? This one's blood is very diluted. His ancestors didn't take advantage of the gift they were given."

Chloe rolled her deep brown eyes. Her lush mouth curved into a wicked grin. "Give him what he needs so he can go after the woman he loves," she instructed.

"You have approval?" Gabriel questioned.

Jack had no idea what they were talking about or whom they really were. A thick current of power and energy flowed around them; suggesting they were more than the typical Mystic he'd run across over the years. The urge to bow before them pressed down hard, but he resisted — barely.

"I don't need approval, Gabriel. Do not forget it was I who brought Thane back into the fold with his lovely Eternal Amara. It is time for you to repay my generosity. I shall consider the debt paid and not bother you again — unless I feel a need." She purred the words at the end and a bolt of sexual tension shot through the air, charging the room.

"You play a dangerous game, Chloe." Gabriel's lips curved into a wicked grin. "I wholly approve. If you win this bet, and after you've had your fun with Eros, come find me and see what it is like to be with a Great Watcher."

Chloe laughed and as quickly as the lust filled the office, it dissipated. "I may take you up on that. Now do get on with it."

"As you wish." Gabriel produced a small vial filled with dark pink liquid from the inside of his long jacket. Uncorking it, he handed it to Jack. "Drink this," the man commanded, a heavy energy pressing him to comply.

Jack took the vial without thought and tossed it back. Whatever he'd just drank was thick and sweet. It raced down his throat, turning into a ball of flame in his stomach before spreading through his limbs. The birthmark on his bicep burned. It was as if a hot branding iron was pressed against him, searing his skin. "Holy shit," he gasped, tossing the vial on the desk. He pushed his sleeve up and what was once a pink-tinged mark was now a filigreed black spear with a pair of angel wings behind it. "What just happened?

What did I just agree to?"

Chloe's husky laughter caressed his ears. "You probably should have asked before drinking the ambrosia. There's no turning back now, my dear Jack."

"Welcome to the fold," Gabriel drawled. "The weak Mystic blood in your body has been strengthened ten fold. Your lifespan is increased and, while you aren't immortal, you will thrive as long as you are with your nymph. That is if you can capture her attention. I've heard the word has gone out in Satyr that a bottled-up nymph is on the prowl. She'll be in high demand, if she so chooses."

Jack's eyes narrowed as rage filled him. "She'll do no such thing," he growled.

"I suggest you go to her then," Chloe said. "You will get immediate access when you show them the Mark of Gabriel on your arm. Good luck, Jack. You have until the end of the month to secure her love. I would hate for you to let me down. There's no telling what would happen to you then." The words sounded like a warning, a threat if he didn't get Lisa's affection. He wasn't worried though. Lisa would be his by the end of the week.

The couple disappeared right before his eyes. The odd warmth and disturbed vision returning to normal as they vanished.

Body numb, he fell into his chair, his mind reeling from what had just taken place. He buzzed his assistant, hoping like hell she would answer him.

"Mrs. French?"

"Yes, Mr. Morgan."

"Have Griff come to my office then join me, please."

"Of course, Mr. Morgan," she responded through the speaker. A couple of minutes later, she walked through the door, followed by his friend.

Hands clasped in front of her, head tipped up a notch, Jack studied the woman. There was a regal air to her. He'd noticed it before, but didn't think anything of it. Wisdom and intellect reflected in her grey-blue eyes. A nudge of awareness filtered into his overwhelmed brain. She wasn't human.

"Did you know what would happen when I called that number, Mrs. French?"

Her eyebrow arched. "I had an idea, Mr. Morgan." Par for the course, she didn't elaborate.

He motioned to the seat in front of his desk. "Would you mind telling me?"

With poise and grace, she sat in the chair, smoothing out her skirt before making eye contact with him. "The number I gave you was to help you in your quest to capture the nymph. I assumed when you called, Chloe would tell you how to go about it."

Jack snorted. It was something like that. "She appeared in my office with a man."

That news seemed to surprise her. "Oh! You were visited by one of the Fates?"

"Is that what she is?"

"I believe Chloe is what she is going by now. What did she want or do with you?"

"The man claimed me as one of his and compelled me to drink…" Jack searched his desk for the vial. Picking it up, he held it out. "To drink a dark pink liquid from this."

Mrs. French gingerly took the vial from his hand and sniffed. A slow grin curled her mouth, taking years off her face. "Ambrosia."

"Yes," he exclaimed. "That's what she called it."

"It is the nectar of the Gods. You've been blessed, sir," she said, her eyes dancing with delight. "What happened when you drank it?"

"I felt like I was on fire on the inside. It started in my chest and traveled out to my arms and legs." He pulled his right sleeve up, showing her the brand in his arm. "My birthmark changed from a faded pink blob to this."

Mrs. French gasped. Her mouth popping open into an exaggerated *O*.

"What is it?" He asked, because he still wasn't too sure.

She reached out and he thought she meant to touch the mark, but she stopped, curling her fingers and drawing away. "You bear the Mark of Gabriel, one of the Great Watchers. You have the blood of an archangel in your veins."

Okay. He vaguely remembered something about archangels, and he'd definitely heard the name Gabriel before. "What does that mean?"

"I'm not sure what you mean?" She said, clearly confused by his question.

"Does this get me closer to what I've wanted for damn near three years?"

Mrs. French laughed lightly. "It does, my dear boy. That mark will open doors you didn't even know existed. Getting into Satyr will not be difficult at all." She stood, bowing slightly before turning to leave.

"One more question, Mrs. French."

She looked at him over her shoulder.

"What type of Mystic are you?"

"I am a Sila. A type of Djinn, or as humans like to call us—a genie."

"I've never heard of a Sila."

"I would expect not. We are rare and while we are meddlesome, we only do it in an attempt to help."

"So you being here wasn't a coincidence."

"Nothing ever is, Mr. Morgan," she said slyly as she walked out the door.

"Wait, Mrs. French, I have…" He trailed off, surprised to see her disappear in a puff of smoke.

"I will never get used to Mystic powers," Griff said, shaking his head.

"I suggest you try. I think I just became one."

CHAPTER SEVEN

April 6th, 6:00pm

SATYR

Jack promised Griff he'd wait until after work to head to Satyr. Their conversation after Mrs. French vanished before their eyes had been…interesting. Griff wasn't as familiar with Mystics. He knew they existed. Knew some worked for them, but he had the more laid back attitude of *what he didn't know, couldn't hurt him.* Jack wanted to blame it on the more sheltered life Griff had growing up, but that could only go so far. He and Griff were thirty. They owned a company together. It was time to open his eyes to the greater world around him.

Now that Jack, for all intents and purposes, was a Mystic; he hoped Griff's attitude would change. That wasn't something Jack could worry about at the moment. He had much more pressing issues to deal with. Like a certain nymph thinking she could give herself to another man.

Climbing into his sleek sports car, he flung his overnight bag into the passenger seat. He made a beeline straight to his condo after his last meeting of the day. Griff knew not to expect him the rest of the week and, thanks to Lisa's insightful scheduling, Jack wasn't actually needed.

Speeding across town, he arrived at Satyr within fifteen minutes. He pulled into the valet parking area, grabbed his bag, handed his valet key over, and took the ticket from the young man drooling over his car. "It'll be here until Friday."

As the man passed by him and uttered *yes sir*, Jack's senses came to life. He smelled the woods after a heavy rain, wet loam and pine; the earthy scents were strong but not overpowering. He turned to look at the kid as he climbed into the car. He was tall, with whipcord leanness to his body. A narrow, long face framed by shaggy brown hair that immediately made him think wolf. Jack shook his head at the vision and made his way inside.

He knew from the many times he'd driven past Satyr that it had two main entrances. One leading to the club, and one leading to the retreat side for the patrons utilizing rooms for overnights or longer periods of time. Jack headed into the retreat side. He figured he'd have a better chance of finding Lisa if he started there.

The huge glass doors slid open silently. As he stepped through, it was like stepping into another world. The lobby was done in elegant shades of deep red and rich dark woods. High ceilings, frescoes, throne chairs, and white marble added to the opulence. Dim lighting and soft music pumped through hidden speakers. And the light scent of lavender wafted through the air.

"Welcome to Retreat Satyr," a distinguished older man greeted him. "If I could see your membership, sir."

"I don't have a membership yet. This is my first time here."

The man sniffed subtly, but it didn't escape Jack's attention. Was he trying to tell by smell if Jack had Mystic in him? "If you'll follow me, please."

The man did an about face, leading Jack down a hall

he hadn't noticed before. They stopped ten feet in. The attendant faced the wall and placed his hand next to a picture of a large oak tree. A secret panel opened silently before him.

They walked into a room with a stout, little man sitting at the desk. "Hello, Henry."

"Mr. Farnsworth, this is the first time the gentleman has been here, and he doesn't have membership."

"I see," Mr. Farnsworth replied. "Are you new to the city or merely visiting?"

"I've lived here my entire life," Jack answered.

Mr. Farnsworth sighed heavily. "Have you come here on a whim? This is a place for Mystics only. No humans allowed."

"I know. My application is being processed."

"Then you know that you must wait until we conclude our investigation before you can come here."

"I do. I talked to the membership liaison earlier in the day. But my circumstances changed this afternoon, and I was told I would get instant access now."

Mr. Farnsworth's thick, white bushy eyebrows rose. "Interesting. Most Mystics know they are one. Our circumstances do not change."

Jack dropped his bag to the floor before pulling up the sleeve on his T-shirt baring his branded bicep. "Mine did."

The little man's eyes popped open wide. He scrambled out of his chair and grabbed something off the floor underneath his desk. He plopped a step stool down in front of Jack and climbed up. His stubby little fingers grabbed hold of Jack's arm, pulling him closer. "This is freshly made," he murmured. "Henry, grab my magnifying glass out of the top drawer, please."

Without taking his eyes off Jack's arm, Mr. Farnsworth snatched the glass from Henry's hand when he brought it over. "Yes, yes," he muttered. "Freshly made. That's why I couldn't tell. The Mark of Gabriel. You're from his blood. Must have been a few generations back."

Mr. Farnsworth climbed off the stool and gathered it up. He walked back to his desk and replaced the step stool before sitting down. "We don't see many of you often. Most descendents with diluted blood don't ever know what they are. You must have pleased the Gods somehow."

Jack didn't know what he'd done to warrant the attention. Was there some kind of crash course he could take on being a Mystic? There had to be rules and regulations they followed. Jack let his thoughts run away from him as he watched the peculiar little man.

Farnsworth unlocked a drawer, before pulling out a sheet of gold paper. He loaded it into a printer then typed away at his computer.

"Place your hand on the pad please," Farnsworth commanded after a few minutes. The upper corner of his desk lit up jerking Jack's attention back to the present.

He did as he was told, placing his hand on the cool metal pad. Seconds later, Jack was handed his new membership card and was following Henry out the hidden door.

"I'll take you to the registration desk, sir. I'm sure they'll have no problem finding you a room."

Jack stopped Henry before they made it there. "Actually, my girlfriend is here for a week and doesn't know I'm here. Honestly, she doesn't know about the Mystic thing either. I haven't had a chance to tell her. I wanted to surprise her. Is there a way we can track her down, maybe send my bag to her room if she's on the Club side?"

Henry grinned wide. "Of course. If you don't mind me asking, what is the lady's name? I should be able to help you out. I've always loved a surprise romantic gesture."

"Lisa Cannon. She's a nymph."

"Ah, I know her. She's a good friend of the manager, Paul. Give me a few minutes while I get the information you need. You'll have your lady friend squealing in delight in no time."

CHAPTER EIGHT

April 6th, 6:30pm

Lisa adjusted the straps on her deep red shift before leaving her room. She'd spent the day relaxing in solitude. Letting her mind and body unwind. Communing with the Goddess and her nymph. It did wonders for her soul. It also gave her time to come to the realization that she and Jack couldn't keep working together. At least, not like they had been the last few years. She'd spent too many hours in his presence, neglecting her inner nymph and allowing her life to be consumed by him. Her determination to keep their relationship strictly professional was in jeopardy if things didn't change.

It was time for her to gain some control. Build up boundaries and insist on a private life. She needed to put a stop to him calling on her twenty-four/seven. When she first started working as his assistant, she made herself completely available. She wanted to ensure he knew she was there whenever he needed her.

Looking back, it had been a huge mistake. They'd both allowed her to become more than *just* an assistant. He leaned on her for everything. Allowing her to be a part of every aspect of his life—except his sex life.

And don't you wish you were a part of that too? Her inner nymph giggled. *She* would have no problem seducing the man. It was a wonder Lisa had been able to hold off as long as she had. She lusted after the man incessantly. Fantasized about him bending her over her desk or his desk. It didn't matter as long as he was the one bringing her to ecstasy. She dreamt of walking over to him while he sat at his desk, climbing on his lap, and fucking the daylights out of him. Day in and day out she was obsessing about him more and more. Imagining them in every sexual position she knew.

She stabbed the button for the elevator, frustrated with the turn of her thoughts. "And that's why I'm here. I need to get a grip on this because it isn't going to happen." She desperately needed to let the nymph free and work her sexual needs out. She couldn't have the man. He was her boss and she actually loved her job. Plus, if she seduced him, ten long years of proving to her family she wasn't a brainless twit using sex to climb the ladder would go down the drain.

The elevator dinged, the doors opening silently. Lavender and lemongrass wafted from the interior. It was meant to soothe and relax some of the more—uptight—patrons, such as demons and other subversive spirits. It did a damn good job of loosening her up as well. Stepping inside she breathed deeply. Her eyes fluttered shut. Tingles raced over her skin, puckering her nipples.

When the car came to a stop on the bottom floor, she swayed slightly. It took a couple of seconds before she could make herself move. Stepping out into the lobby she hooked a right, heading to the interior club entrance. Pressing her hand against the pad embedded in the wall, the large, soundproof leather-studded door opened.

Quickly heading into the club, the door swooshed closed behind her. Her eyes adjusted to the dim lighting in a matter of seconds. People milled about in various states of dress and forms. The music was soft, atmosphere one of relaxed decadence. It was the calm before the storm, a way to get the patrons loose before moving into the room further.

There were three levels to Club Satyr. The main one in which she stood, served food and drinks, and had places to lounge, mingle, and talk. Moving away from the entrances and deeper into the room, there were a couple of stages for dancing. Beyond those, there were three large rooms for open play. Mystics looking to enjoy a more self-indulgent ambience could watch or participate in whatever was going on…as long as the partners were agreeable.

The lower level was where demons and those interested in the darker persuasions would go to mingle and play. Also, there was a large seating area and patrons could reserve one of six rooms, two being dungeons.

The upper levels reminded her of the retreat side of Satyr. They boasted long hallways that branched off into multiple rooms. Like the lower level, the rooms could be reserved at the bar and used for whatever purpose a guest could imagine. If someone had a special request or specific theme, then that could also be arranged.

It had been so long since Lisa had been at Satyr, she thought she'd hang out on the main level and do a little people watching. Making her way to the bar, she ordered an Elixir de Menthe. A honey, mint, and water cocktail. The bartender had her scan her palm so her tab would be billed to her room.

She found an empty chair near the public play area and sat back sipping her drink. The sweet minty concoction went down her throat smoothly, the burn settling in her belly before flowing through her veins.

She breathed in the heady scent of sex and pheromones, while bodies gyrated ten feet from her. A fairy flitted past with a wolf in tow, a thick black studded collar around his neck, the leash hanging from the fairy's hand. The giant brown beast's tongue lolling out of his mouth, its eyes focused on the delicate creature leading him. When they reached the edge of the play area, the wolf shifted into a bulky six-foot man. Dark brown hair flowed down his naked back, swishing above his firm ass.

A couple of minutes after watching the fairy and wolf go by, the man who served her lunch approached. He wore the same tight leather pants and no top. Why would he? His tips were probably fantastic…whether monetary or physical. He really did have a fabulous body.

His grin was slow to take as he ran his gaze over her. "If it isn't my afternoon tip. You know it's been months since anyone has turned me down."

She wasn't surprised. "It must have been a shock," she quipped. It had been a shock to her that she hadn't taken him up on his offer. He would be the perfect specimen in her quest to start working Jack from her system.

"A slight one. But then I'd hoped to see you again and change your mind." He motioned to the empty seat next to her, silently asking if anyone was sitting there.

She didn't hesitate this time, her resolve to push Jack from her mind at the forefront. "Please, do." She took another sip of her cocktail. Fascinated as he lowered his massive body into the chair. He stretched his tree trunk thighs out in front of him. The leather molded to them, showing off the power within. She waited for a flare of arousal to spark and the nymph to take the lead. She was disappointed when nothing happened.

"Thank you," he rumbled. "I have to ask, what is a woman like you doing in a place like this?"

A burst of laughter broke free of her chest unbidden. "That is the cheesiest line…*ever*."

He shrugged. "It's an honest question. I'm going to guess you're a sprite, elf, or…" he raked a heated gaze over her then grinned, "a nymph."

"Ding, ding, ding. I'm a nymph. One who doesn't get out as much as she'd like. Which explains why I'm here. What about you? You're awfully…" she paused and licked her lips, "big." Just because she didn't feel arousal, it didn't mean she didn't appreciate his form.

"What would be your guess?" He asked smoothly, leaning forward as if he were giving her a better view to decide.

She took a moment to catalogue his features. He was a beautiful man: Dark skin. Sculpted physique. Devastating bright, white smile and mischievous eyes with inherent strength oozing from him. Incredible sexual allure that had passersby taking a second and sometimes third glance. There was also a spiritual power vibrating around him. "My best guess," narrowing her eyes she raked his body again. If only she felt a flicker of something. "Centaur."

"Very good," he said leaning back. "Would you like another?" he asked, motioning to her glass.

She hadn't been aware she'd finished the first. It was on the tip of her tongue to say yes when a figure appeared behind her companion. "No, she would not," the new man growled.

It can't be. She knew that voice, even with the anger threading through it. Her gaze was drawn to Jack, sending her heart into palpitations. He was a man who demanded her attention without even trying, like a sexy pair of heels whispering her name from her favorite store's display. He was the drug she was trying to give up. She ogled him, skimming over his thick chest, his T-shirt clinging to the muscles beneath. Her breath caught in her throat, arousal pooled low in her belly, erasing the warmth from the alcohol and replacing it with something much more devastating. She never saw him wearing a T-shirt. Not even the nights he called her to his condo for last-minute work or to help with something. It was always a crisp dress shirt and slacks. This new casual look slayed her good intentions.

She swallowed hard when her gaze collided with his. Anger did indeed burn bright in his dark brown orbs. A buzzing started in her ears and her head spun. She'd never had that reaction to him before.

"Lisa," her companion in the chair beside her said, his voice full of concern. She blinked repeatedly, dragging herself from the fog that descended around her. It was odd to hear her name fall from his lips. She assumed he got it from the delivery ticket, she'd certainly never told him. She snorted when she realized she didn't even remember his.

"I'm sorry," she said, directing it to the man. "My boss is behind you, it must be something important if he's shown up here." She stood, holding out her hand. "It was nice to see you again."

He stood without comment, tipping his head down marginally. Taking her hand, he kissed the back of it then walked away. The anger from Jack blasted her, damn near knocking her back. She almost called the man back to be a buffer between her and her boss.

Her boss...her *human* boss stood in the middle of the club staring at her as if she'd done something wrong. Her lust drained away, anger taking its place. "How the hell did you get in here?"

"What did you mean, *nice to see you again*?" He came around the chair, stepping into her personal space. Fury vibrated off him, along with something else she couldn't identify. He was too close, messing up her senses. This was supposed to be her time to purge him from her mind. From her fantasies. Not have him show up and tempt her to let loose.

She opened her mouth, then closed it again without any words coming out. She was stunned by his arrival and incredibly aroused...even angry. At the mere sight of him in this place, her miniscule panties dampened and her pussy convulsed.

The nymph was a devil on her shoulder, tempting her to touch. To take what she so desperately wanted deep inside.

Jack stared down into the face of the woman he wanted as desperately as his next breath. She was shocked. He could see it written over her delicate features as plain as day. It was essential to his state of mind he get her out of the club and someplace where no one would interrupt them. Preferably to her room. He needed her alone, no distractions, until she agreed to be his forever.

His body shook with fury and a strong desire to pulverize the man who had been sitting with her. Chatting her up. Making her laugh. No man had the right to do that. No man but him.

It had been so long since he'd heard that full, throaty sound. The one that reached down and grabbed him by the balls. The time to hold back and keep a grip on the employer/employee relationship had passed. He needed more. Snaking an arm around her, he pulled her to him. He gripped her chin, angling her head to keep her in place, then pressed the first of what would become many kisses to her lips. He devoured her. The rough penetration with his tongue into her mouth a testament to how little control he currently had. He used everything in his arsenal to seduce her: his teeth, his tongue, and his lips. He nipped, sucked, and reveled in her quick fiery response. Her tongued tangled with his and she pressed her body closer. His dick pulsed to life against her flat stomach.

She tasted so damn good. The mint of whatever drink she'd had and the sweet carnal taste of her nymph rolling to the surface. He could sense that part of her now. Feel it calling out to his newly enhanced blood. If only he'd been able to become a Mystic sooner.

A hand landed on his ass jolting him into awareness. Lisa's hands were curled into the front of his shirt. There was no way her hand was on his ass. He was reluctant to break their connection. His need to feast on her becoming a living, breathing creature demanding satisfaction. But something

60

wasn't right. Turning his head, there was a slim, willowy woman crowding into their space. She grinned and flashed sharp pointed teeth.

"No," he growled and peeled Lisa's hands from his chest. Threading their fingers together, he pulled her toward the retreat side and away from the interloper. She came along without protest; hopefully, still too dazed to realize what was going on. It was a minor victory he would relish later.

"Where are we going?" She asked breathlessly as they weaved between people.

"Your room."

"My room?" She chirped.

"Yes, unless you want to stay here and have everyone watch as I fuck you senseless and claim you as mine."

Her eyebrows shot up in surprise. She blinked a couple of times and he knew his words were sinking in. "Oh! Um," she looked around frantically, "no. We'll go upstairs."

Jack powered his way through the club and back to the retreat side. They paused at the bank of elevators waiting for the car to arrive.

Her quiet voice broke the silence around them. "How did you even get in? Humans are banned unless by special invitation."

He had no intention of talking about what transpired earlier in his office in a public setting. He may be in the world of the Mystics, but he figured even his experience was outside their norm. The elevator finally arrived and opened, he steered her in, finger hovering over the panel.

"Eight," she said dazed.

They rode up, hands linked together. It was heaven to

finally touch her like he'd always wanted. To feel her soft, delicate hand in his. It was such a simple sign of affection and he fucking loved it.

The elevator arrived on her floor without any stops. They stepped out and he allowed her to lead the way. She had the last room on the right. The door tucked away in the corner. Pressing her hand to a panel next to it, the door opened.

The designer in him was floored by the technology he'd seen so far. The overprotective man in him was pleased to know no one could get in without scanning his or her palm. An added sense of security he would need to check into later. He'd also need to get his print added to her room code in case they ever decided to leave the room again. He didn't plan on it, but he wasn't adverse if it meant moving from their room to a playroom.

All of that could wait until later. Top priority in his feverish brain was pinning her against the nearest flat surface and staking his claim.

Lisa whirled on him as soon as the door shut. He reached out, tugging her toward him, wrapping his arms around her. Her soft little curves pressed into him. Before she could blast him for manhandling her, he bent his head and fed on her kissable lips. She mewled in response when his tongue swept inside, wrapping around hers.

Her adept fingers threaded into his hair, gripping it, tugging him close. He sure as hell wasn't going to resist. He could tell she wanted him as badly as he wanted her. He'd have to be a complete idiot not to take what she was offering.

He lifted her off the floor, blindly making it to the bed. He spun and sat, arranging her until she straddled him. The soft center of her body landed on his jean-clad dick. It jerked in his pants, causing a bite of pain to shoot into his balls. In an odd twist, it brought him back in check, helping him gain a modicum of control.

She nipped his lip, making him pull back slightly. "Mr. Morgan, we can't."

"Don't Mr. Morgan me, and we can," he growled. Nipping her back. "You'll call me Jack from here on out. Unless of course it turns you on to call me Mr. Morgan or sir."

Lisa ground her hips down, pulling a moan from him. "Jack," she purred softly and he damn near came in his pants. "What do you think you're doing here?"

"I thought I was kissing you. I must not have been doing a good enough job if you couldn't figure that out."

She leaned in and licked his upper lip. "You were doing fine. What are you doing at Satyr? You can't be here. You aren't a Mystic. They'll punish you if they see you." Panic laced her voice, and he couldn't help but smile. He liked knowing she was concerned for him.

"It'll be fine, trust me. We'll talk about that later. I've waited too long for this." Standing with her clinging tightly to him, he turned them around. She gasped, clutching him harder as he crawled up the bed, his arm wrapped around her waist to keep her anchored in place.

Settling her on the bed, he peppered kisses over her face and down her neck to her shoulder. Her soft skin was like silk beneath his lips. Soft, smooth, and luxurious. He wanted every inch of her rubbing against every inch of him. He tugged at the flimsy strap holding her dress up, snapping it easily. He gave the other side the same treatment before yanking the dress down her slim body. Inch by quick inch, the body he'd dreamed about was revealed. Her firm, perky little breasts with dark brown puckered nipples entered his view. He scraped his thumbs over the tips lightly. She gasped and arched, silently begging for more attention.

Not one to deny her, he sucked one tip into his mouth. Worrying the nub against the roof. As he drew off, he clamped his teeth down and tugged. She squealed and he popped off, giving the other nipple to the same treatment.

Her fingers threaded back into his hair, pulling and yanking on the dark strands as he applied sweet torture to her other breast. He didn't linger. There was more he wanted to do before he sunk his cock into her. He skimmed down the center of her body, pulling the dress as he went. Sitting up, he tugged the damn thing off along with her thong. Tired of playing with the fabric impeding his view of her beautiful body.

When he looked down to take in the sight, he didn't stop the growl bursting free. She was spread out like a feast. A bevy of delicacies waiting to be devoured. He vowed to taste every inch of her before their time at Satyr was up. Prove his case that they were meant to be together forever. A well-oiled machine at work and explosive pair in private. A true powerhouse couple.

Lisa looked through dazed eyes up at Jack. His dark stubbled jaw, his mouth pulled into a taut line. Fire sparked in the depths of his deep brown eyes. At the moment, she didn't care that he was her boss and she his employee. She'd lusted after him for years, and it seemed they had a mutual desire. Plus, the second she'd seen him, angry and pulsing with hot desire, she gave into her deepest wish. She promised herself whatever happened at Satyr, would stay at Satyr. She would have to lay down ground rules later. After she sated her overwhelming need to have him thrusting deep inside her body, rocking her to orgasm.

Her nymph pulled free, bursting to the surface. Her inhibitions melted and all thoughts were centered on the man working his way down her body. Dark cravings hammered within her and demanded more of his sensual assault. She wanted him to take her on every possible surface, in every possible way. She wanted to be pushed down to her knees and made to suck his cock. To be taken roughly from behind. To have her ass dominated and her pussy spanked. Every dirty little thing her nymph could think of, Lisa wanted to do with this man and only him.

Jack reached out and ran one of his thick digits over the slick folds of her pussy. "So wet, baby," he whispered, his eyes fastened to her nearly clean-shaven crotch. He pushed a finger between the swollen lips, dipping into her core slightly. As he pulled it out, he ran it over her clit, drawing a moan from her lips. The man undid her with a simple touch.

Her pussy throbbed and juices flowed as he stuck his finger in his mouth, licking her flavor away. "Mmm," he moaned, "delicious. Just like I knew it would be."

Wedging his shoulders between her legs, he placed his hands on the backs of her thighs, giving him better access. Eyes glittering with lust, he dipped his tongue in before flicking up and over her clit. Lick after lick he did the same thing, driving her to the edge of madness.

Feet tingling, the pinpricks of sensation worked up her body, twisting her arousal into something more, waiting to explode. Grabbing his hair she tugged hard, attempting to pull him away. She wanted to come but refused to do so without his cock driving her over the edge. Without her pussy clamping down on his thick, steely erection as he pounded into her.

Jack must have gotten the hint. He stood and dropped his jeans to the ground, his hard cock bouncing against his stomach. Long and thick, it curved toward his belly.

Her eyes grew wide and she wondered why she'd never noticed how damn big he was before. Probably because she'd been too mesmerized by his handsome face, his dark eyes as they glittered with some unknown emotion. She licked her dry lips in anticipation. The longing to have him gliding his hard length in and out of her mouth a physical need. She could practically feel what the ridges of the veins running along his shaft would feel like, giving her something to tease and stroke.

"Later," Jack grunted as he lowered himself over her body. He bent her legs, pushing them up against her chest, giving him a direct view of her wet pussy. He thrust forward, impaling her on his cock. The sudden movement pulled a cry from her throat. Sharp movements in and out helped her stretch and adjust to his width. It had been forever since she'd been with a man. Since she'd felt the need that curled around her, hurling her into the erotic tug of war.

Just because her nymph grabbed hold, it didn't mean she'd forgotten about disease and pregnancy. While Mystics were generally disease free—you never knew about some demons—humans were a different matter altogether.

Humans unknowingly had the ability to infect or impregnate a Mystic. Their biology makeup was intended to further the Mystic races. A defense created by the Gods to combat extinction.

"Protection," she squeaked, pressing her hands hard against his chest. Her legs, though, weren't on board; she locked them around his waist as if afraid he would move too far away. Her body was a contradiction of wants and needs

Jack dropped his forehead onto hers. "Damn," he breathed harshly. "I'm clean but for you I'll do anything." He pulled out and fumbled with his jeans. Coming up with a condom, he opened and rolled it on in less than a second.

She'd never had a man say that to her. They'd always tried to convince her it would be fine and promise to pull out or some other ridiculous thing. Being a nymph didn't mean she was a pushover when it came to sex. She was desperate to fill every sexual craving coursing through her at the time.

He pushed back in, tugging on the swollen tissues of her pussy. It dragged her back to the present. "Been so damn long," he panted, rocking into her. "Been waiting…for you."

"Oh." The confession shocked her. She tried not to pay attention to Jack's love life or lack of one. He wasn't one of those bosses that leaned on her to buy gifts for his current flavor of the week. And when she thought about it, his dates had become few and far between.

"Lisa," he said. "Are you with me?"

She pulled his head down and kissed him roughly. "Yes, Jack. Fuck me, please."

Jack sat back, kneeling between her spread thighs. He skated his hands over her hips, moving them beneath her body until he gripped her ass. He tilted her pelvis higher and fucked her in long, drawn out thrusts. "Damn, baby. I've needed you so badly."

"Yes!"

His paced picked up with each breathy moan she let loose. Each hard drive into her body electrifying her nerve endings until she was awash in sensation. Soon he rode her hard. His cock pounding in and out of her pussy, smacking against her clit and shoving her arousal even higher.

She tilted her head back, panting as stroke after stroke created a wave of pleasure unlike any she'd felt before. She was close to orgasm. But needed something to push her over the edge.

As if reading her thoughts, Jack leaned over her body, sucking a nipple into his mouth. He pulled on it hard with his teeth before laving it. Moving to the other side he did it again, the rough sucking and bite at the end, only this time her body shook with her impending orgasm. It rolled over her like a tsunami. Her back bowed off the bed as a strangled scream left her lips.

Jack powered into her, extending her orgasm, her pussy doing its damndest to keep a grip on his turgid flesh. He released her breast and captured her lips, swallowing down her cries. In a frenzied rush, he used her body until he tumbled over the edge. He lifted his head and shouted her name. His cock jerking as he came hard. She felt the heat of his release through the thin layer of the condom; suddenly regretting having him put one on.

Jack rolled to the side, pulling her with him. They stayed entwined together, both breathing deeply. A fine sheen of sweat covered him. The nymph was pleased he worked hard to help them both achieve pleasure.

CHAPTER NINE

April 6th, 10:00pm

Lisa rolled over, her hand coming in contact with Jack's extremely warm, hard body. Dancing her fingers over his smooth chest, she sighed in contentment. She'd finally gotten a taste of her fantasy. Jack fucking her as if she were the only woman he'd ever wanted.

"What was that sigh for?" He rumbled, stroking a hand lightly down her back.

Her fingers drifted to one of his nipples. Flickering and pinching it lightly. "Nothing."

He chuckled, the vibration seeping into her. The sound matching her contentment and, dare she say, happiness. "I doubt that. No woman ever makes that sound without a meaning behind it."

"I don't think now is the best time to talk about other women, do you?" She ran her hand down the middle of his chest, heading straight for his cock. She took him in hand, stroking delicately over the hardening flesh. She ghosted her thumb over the slit, gathering the pre-cum pearled on the tip. She was torn between removing her hand completely to lick the salty-goodness off and crawling between his thighs to sample from the source.

Sampling from the source won out. Flinging back the sheet he had covered them with when he'd gotten rid of his condom, she moved between his legs. "Hands behind your head," she said with a bit of steel threading her voice. One of her favorite things to do to a man was to make it impossible for him to touch. Allow him to concentrate on the feeling of her lips wrapped about his hard member and not worry about pleasing her. She'd prefer to have his hands tied to the bedposts using his ties, but she would compromise this one time. They could play that fantasy out later. "No, moving them. You do and I stop. This is my treat and your pleasure."

Jack did as he was told and a low, rumbling groan emerged from his throat when she leaned over and licked the tip. She fondled his balls, pressing on the smooth space directly behind them. His hips popped off the bed, thrusting his dick between her lips.

She swirled her tongue around the spongy head. Sucking lightly on it before running her tongue over, around and up his length again. Gripping the base, she held him straight up before leaning over him and taking him completely to the back of her throat. She swallowed and he grunted, his hand landing on her head before she could do anything else.

She popped off and sat back. "Nah, ah, ah," she tsked.

His face was flushed, his arousal painted across his tanned cheeks. He placed his hand beneath his head again.

"Do it again and I'm done. That was your one and only warning."

Jack nodded sharply.

Placing her hands on his hips to keep them in place, she

sucked the length back inside her hot mouth.

Bobbing up and down, she regulated the pace; keeping to a steady rhythm that she knew would pull him to the edge but not push him over.

Jack tried powering up, pushing his hips against her small hands. He probably thought he'd be able to force his will and need on her. Too bad he didn't realize the strength she possessed as a nymph. She was no delicate flower, easily shoved around.

Jack didn't know how he'd gotten so damn lucky. Lisa hovered over his dick sucking it like the last lollipop she'd ever get. She swallowed him down deeper and deeper. Her throat closing over the end in a heated kiss.

The wet heat of her mouth drove him insane. The desire to tangle his fingers in her dark hair, to dominate her and shove his dick harder and faster down her throat, nearly broke him. He knew he had a white knuckled grip on his hands to keep them in place.

His hips bounced slightly off the bed, something he knew she was doing, not him. It stunned him for a moment when she'd held him down with little effort. Point made, he concentrated on keeping them still.

She moaned in the back of her throat. One of her small hands cupped his balls as a finger from her other hand slid over the smooth spot behind them and worked its way into his crack. She brushed over his ass hole and he jerked, the sensation from her soft exploration completely unexpected.

Wiggling her finger, she pressed inside the tight ring of his ass, sliding it in and out with tiny thrusts.

It was too much. His release rushed forward, his balls pulling up firmly against his body. "Gonna come," he huffed out in warning.

Lisa wasn't put off. She shoved the finger in his ass

deeper and swallowed around the head of his dick. His back arched and his cock convulsed. He roared as he emptied himself down her throat. Black spots dotted his vision and he swore he would pass out from lack of oxygen.

Coming off him with a pop, Lisa licked the head of his rapidly softening dick. She removed her finger from his ass, and then crawled up his body. Before he could react, she kissed him hard and quick, then rolled off the side of the bed.

"I'll be right back, lover," she called out as she went into the bathroom.

Lisa walked out of the bathroom to find Jack in the exact same position she she'd left him. Sprawled out and sated. She chuckled and climbed onto the bed with him, sitting cross-legged next to him.

"How you feeling?" She reached toward the bottom of the bed and pulled the covers up over them.

"Like I've died and gone to heaven," he murmured.

"I'll take that as a good thing."

"Oh yeah," he drawled, a smile curving his sexy mouth. Her heart flipped and her tummy took flight. The man devastated her good intentions. The past three years she'd worked hard to keep things professional and in one extremely good hour it had been obliterated. She wasn't sure she minded though. Good thing she'd decided to treat this encounter like a trip to Vegas.

Jack pushed to a sitting position, his back against the headboard. "Since you didn't come lay back down, I'm guessing we aren't going to sleep."

She shook her head. Now that she'd gotten two fantasies out of the way, her nymph wanted more. First, though, they needed to have *the talk*.

Jack put his hand on her knee and started to rub up and down her thigh. The closer he got to her pussy, the more her arousal sparked. She could imagine what those long, thick fingers could do to her. How they would feel thrusting into her cunt, hitting just the right spot to set her off.

Add another thing to the to-do list. "I was thinking we could order some food and have a little chat. You need to explain a few things, and we need to set some ground rules."

"Ground rules," he uttered through clenched teeth. His good-natured smile vanished. He certainly didn't like the sound of that, but it was too damn bad. Whatever was going on between them couldn't last.

Boss. Employee. All day, practically every day. That screamed bad news—for her.

"Yes, ground rules. Before we get into them, let's get food. You're going to need your strength later," she said suggestively.

CHAPTER TEN

April 6th, 11:00pm

Jack stood at the door as he waited for the attendant with the cart to leave. The second the man walked through the door, Jack had been on edge. Tension vibrated through his body and he fought to keep his cool.

The man stared at Lisa like she was the prize at the bottom of the cereal box. While Jack agreed with that idea, Lisa was *his* prize and he had no intention of sharing. He wanted to tuck her away from the world; never letting another human being set eyes on her.

Logically he knew she would never go for it, but it didn't stop him from picturing it in his head. Just like it didn't stop him from imagining throwing the man out the window because he was leering at Lisa.

The man eventually took the hint, rolling the cart through the open door. Jack slammed it behind him, not bothering to tip him. The man got a good look at Jack's woman and that had been enough.

"Are you going to join me or continue scowling because that man had the audacity to look at me?" She chuckled and sat down.

Jack grunted and joined her at the small table next to the window. "If it'd been up to me, he never would have entered the room."

"You can't always have your way."

"Who says?"

She laughed and popped a grape into her mouth. "Me."

They ate their food, talking about everything but her silly rules idea. It pissed him off she wanted ground rules, but seeing as how they never talked about what was going on between them, he grudgingly understood.

Lisa pushed her empty plate away and looked at him. He took a sip of water as he waited for her to start. His ground rules consisted of her being with him and only him — and no man ever touching her again.

"So," she said, tapping her manicured nails on the table.

"Yes." He leaned back and crossed his arms over his chest. He knew whatever rules she came up with he wouldn't like. Knew she would put restrictions on their relationship. Time limits. Things they could and could not do together. He'd agree for the moment if it meant he got to spend time with her. It would give him time to lure her to his way of thinking.

She licked her lips and pulled in a breath. "The ground rules."

"I don't think we need them." It didn't hurt to make an opening volley of what he wanted.

Her lush little mouth opened before snapping shut. Lips pinching like she'd sucked on a lemon. "We do. We work together. We can't let whatever we do here change what we have out there."

His eyes narrowed. "I think the changes in here will only make out there better. I want more than one night. I *will* have more than one night." He wanted — needed — every night, but now wasn't the time to tell her that.

She considered him for a moment, eyes narrowed, lips pursed, before her face cleared. A small smile edging onto her face. "Okay. I'd like that too."

He let a slow grin curl one corner of his mouth. It was a tiny win. One he'd take. "Good," he said with deep satisfaction.

"I'm here for a week. Like I originally planned." Her eyebrow rose, daring him to comment.

He wouldn't. Now wasn't the time to admit he'd done it because he was jealous. Well, there was never a time to admit that. He was a man after all. "I've decided to take the week off as well."

"With your schedule that shouldn't be a problem. I'm sure Mr. Powers can handle anything that comes up. He's got Janet if he can't."

"I agree. I'm sure you arranged it that way. For the record, I *can* take care of myself."

She chuckled lightly. "I wonder sometimes."

"You don't need to. I'm really good at taking care of things that are important to me." He reached out and captured her hand. Hoping his double meaning would sink in.

"I'm sure you are. The company is still thriving and the plant in your house isn't dead, last I checked."

The slightly brown ficus tree she gave him came to

mind. Now probably wouldn't be a good time to mention he hadn't watered it in a while. He cleared his throat and steered his mind back to the conversation. "What are your ground rules?"

"First, answer me this. Is your wanting me a new thing?"

"Nope. I've wanted you since the first day I met you." There was no sense in not telling her the truth. He'd have to backtrack later if he lied. Not how he wanted to start things off.

"When I walked through the door to be your temp?"

Jack thought back to that day. He remembered it vividly. Her hair was cut much like it was at the moment. A short, straight bob parted to one side. Deep red glossy lipstick on her lush lips that begged for a kiss. She wore a charcoal grey jacket over a white silk shirt, a matching grey skirt with a black patent bow accenting her tiny waist, and the most badass deep red heels that screamed fuck-me. He'd been stunned and hooked on the spot. "Sounds about right."

She blinked a couple times. "Huh, okay. So, what we did not too long ago is something you've wanted for a while?"

"Yes, and I plan on doing it again — and again — and again."

Lisa visibly gulped. Her head bobbed and eyes grew big. "A week," she blurted out. "We can indulge in our attraction this week only. After we get back to the real world, we go back to employee," she pointed to herself, "and boss," she pointed to him.

It was on the tip of his tongue to say no. It wasn't even close to what he wanted. But he'd convince her. "Is that it?"

"No. You're exclusive with me while you're here. There are a lot of temptations around, and I don't want you getting distracted."

He tugged on her hand and pulled her over to him. She landed in his lap easily. Her arms wrapping around his neck. "I wouldn't have it any other way."

She huffed out a breath and relaxed into him. "How did you get in here anyway? They're pretty strict."

Jack held out his left arm to show her the strange tattoo.

She lifted a finger and traced over it making him shudder. Her light touch provoked an unfamiliar feeling to shoot through him. The mark warmed and his body tingled. His heart sped up, thumping wildly in his chest.

"When did you get this?"

"Believe it or not, I've always had it. Well, not exactly like this. Before it was more of a faint pink blob and if you looked closely, it was shaped the same. This afternoon a man and a woman magically appeared in my office after I called a number your replacement gave me. The man looked at the birthmark and declared I was one of his. He compelled me to drink some sweet liquid from a small vial that burned through my veins, and then my birthmark turned into this. When I showed it to the little man downstairs, he gave me VIP access and instant access."

"The little man?"

"Mr. Farnsworth. I don't know what he is. He kind of reminded me of a dwarf. I really don't know much about the Mystic world, other than you are part of it and I hoped I was somehow. I applied to Satyr a long time ago, but they only found a distant relative to an angel that they couldn't confirm."

"Wait. An angel?" She grabbed his arm and studied it closer. "This is the Mark of Gabriel. You're a descendent of a Great Watcher?"

Jack shrugged, "That's the name Chloe called him by."

"Chloe? She's one of the Fates. She decides life. If anyone can change the course of someone's destiny, then it would be her."

"If you say so. I feel like I need a crash course in all things Mystic."

She bussed his lips quickly. "I'll help you out. Actually, Satyr is the perfect place to learn a few things. To get a feel for what the Mystic world is like."

Jumping up off his lap, she went to the dresser. Grabbing out a short leather skirt and tiny tank top, she pulled them on, dropping her robe to the floor. "Put a shirt on and we'll go downstairs for a bit. Its late enough we should be able to find something interesting going on. Mondays are slow, so you won't be overwhelmed."

Lisa strapped her feet into sky-high heels that had him drooling as he put on the T-shirt he discarded earlier. Fuck, she was sexy as hell. Visions of fucking her while she wore the shoes and nothing else flitted through his head.

She took his hand and tugged him to the door. "Let's go play." She winked and they left the room.

CHAPTER ELEVEN

April 7th, 1:00am

Lisa twirled on the dance floor; safe in the knowledge that no one would bother her. Her brooding boss and temporary lover sat five feet away watching her have the time of her life. She tried to lure him out with her but he declined, saying something ridiculous about not having any rhythm.

If he'd bothered to look around, he'd see it really didn't matter. There were sirens shimmying and shaking parts that shouldn't move, at least not in public. A couple of Psy-vamps hovered near the edge feeding off the lust spilling from the woman.

There was a group of fairies swaying to the loud thumping music, knocking back honeyed drinks. One looked to be a bride, a wreath of flowers atop her head, a tiny veil hanging down her back.

Lisa danced her way over to Jack, snagging his gaze to make sure he was watching. Sliding her hands down her sides seductively, she poured on the charm, using all of the skills of her nymph. Hips gyrating like a belly dancer. Hands caressing her flesh. She let her body call to him.

She'd forgone any type of underwear, wanting that bit of freedom, that easy access just in case. Her arousal coated the insides of her thighs, her pussy clenching rhythmically at the thought of climbing on Jack's lap and fucking him where he sat.

It wouldn't be the first time that had happened at the club. It was known for looser inhibitions. The deeper a person went inside, the more depraved it become. She wanted Jack to see the world he'd just entered. The lusty, sexual, anything goes side.

Lisa stopped in front of him, her pussy level with his face. The heels she wore adding the right amount of height to her short frame.

Jack leaned forward and grabbed her hips. He pulled her in close, brushing soft kisses over her taut stomach. When he pulled back and looked up at her, his eyes were filled with desire.

She knew just the place to let that desire flow. On a Monday night there shouldn't be very many people there, but enough to play into her voyeuristic side. "Let's go. I want to show you something."

Jack stood and took her hand into his. A thrill skittered up her spine at the simple touch of fingers lacing together. It was possessive and intimate. Connected them in a manner that made her heart skip a beat.

She guided him through the club to a set of elevators tucked away in the back.
The doors opened as soon as they stepped in front of them and then boarded. She pressed the button for the lower level.

It took a couple seconds to reach the bottom floor. Stepping out into a dimly light open area, the scent of sex and magic washed over them, stirring her magical blood.

A few couples were scattered in the different seating areas. Most in some sexual position.

Lisa took Jack over to the first door on the left. The voyeur window was closed, so she moved them along. "There are six rooms down here and, as you see, a giant open area. Each of the rooms has the ability to become an open viewing room, a closed private room, or be divided into two rooms for more private occupancy. Two of the rooms," she pointed to the door they first stopped at and then down to the other end, "are dungeons, BDSM or medieval, whatever catches the users fancy. Demons typically reserve the rooms months in advance and they're very difficult to get."

They stopped in front of another room. "The remaining four rooms are like this one." They peered into the window. The heavy black curtains had been pulled back and there was a centaur in full form walking around a pixie splayed on the bed in the middle of the room. His long black hair flowed down his back. His muscular chest gleamed with sweat.

Jack stiffened next to her for a split second. "That's a…" he broke off.

She smiled and continued. "You can move the furniture around to your liking. There are new, packaged toys if you want to use them. After you're done using the room, its cleaned and the attendant will gather any used toys, clean them and charge them to your room. They'll be delivered later or you can pick them up at check-out."

Jack looked down into her face, eyebrow raised in question.

"Yes, he's a centaur. But don't go thinking Mystics are weird or anything. They won't have sex while he's in that form. The people who come down here are more into exhibitionism and some of the darker kinks. Some Mystics need more than what the human realm can provide. We come here to work through our fantasies or needs. Take a break from the real world or connect with others of our kind."

"And what was your plan when you booked your week?"

They turned from the room and found an empty couch against the back wall. Jack sat and pulled her down with him. They could still see inside the open room. The centaur pulled a long black feather along the pixie's body, making her squirm. She panted and white sparkles shot from her hands.

Lisa turned to face Jack, pulling her legs under her. Running her hand over his broad chest, she played with his nipples in hopes to distract him or at least keep her focused while she exposed a little of her soul. "Do you want my honest answer or the one you *think* you want to hear?"

Jack canted his head and looked at her through narrowed eyes. "The honest answer, of course."

"I came here to work you out of my system." She knew she shouldn't tell him, but she couldn't help herself. A part of her, way back in the area of her brain that had no business chiming in, wanted him to know she'd been lusting after him too. That the silly romantic in her hoped they could turn the week into something more. It wasn't a good idea or logical but neither was that part of her.

Jack grinned and pulled her onto his lap. She straddled his thick thighs, the short leather skirt riding up. "Kind of hard to work me out of your system without me here." His fingers dug into her hips, pressing her against his hard erection. She gasped at the contact and couldn't help rocking her hips.

"I had a substitute," she confessed, her voice breathy.

"Absolutely not," he growled and thrust up. "Ain't nothing like the real thing, baby."

"I...I...." she stuttered. What could she say? "I would

have made do. He wouldn't have cared if I'd imagined someone else or screamed your name. Part of his job is to morph into the client's deepest desire. It didn't matter after you cancelled my plans. He went to the next person on the waiting list."

"Did you know he wasn't available when you came?"

"Yes, Paul told me. But I had to come. I couldn't stand it in the office anymore. I've wanted you for so long, and my nymph pushed harder and harder to break free. You don't know what its been like for me, hiding what I am all of the time."

Jack was quick to cut her off. "I never told you to do that."

She chuckled sadly. "No, it was my decision years ago. I let her out when it becomes too much. I come to Satyr and feed the nymph, then I go back to the real world. The world I love. You've been cancelling my plans a lot and this had to be done."

"You're aren't doing it without me. Not anymore."

A smile curved the corner of her mouth. Jack said it with such conviction, as if he'd be there for more than just the stolen week they were having. She couldn't go around believing in the fairy tale though. It would lead to trouble down the road. Especially when he got tired of her and her nymph-y ways. Or when he was forced to meet the people she called family. Flighty and flirty, that describes just about all of them. And the reason she kept that corner of her life locked away.

No, now wasn't the time to head down that line of thought. Her time with Jack was temporary. They would never get to the point he had to meet her family. It was time to make them both forget what the hell they were talking about and focus back on the reason they were in the downstairs club.

84

She pressed her lips against his, taking her time. Flicking her tongue along the seam of his mouth, he opened and she dove in. Tongues tangled and mated, for minutes on end. Breaking contact, she puffed across his lips, "At least not this week. That's all I need." *Until next time.* She wouldn't worry about it right now. She had a sinfully hot man between her legs. Sex and magic filled the air around them. And the centaur and pixie were putting on a show that made her wish she was the one tied down and Jack was stalking around her deciding what debauched thing to do next.

"We'll see about that," Jack said cryptically. He glanced around at the other people in the room. No one seemed to care that people could watch them make out or even have sex. The couple a few feet away proved that. They were both naked; the man's head tipped back resting on the back of the plush chair as the woman knelt between his feet bobbing up and down on his shaft.

As if he felt the weight of Jack's stare, the man lifted his head and made eye contact. Except it wasn't a set of human eyes staring back at him. His eyes glowed a deep red. His mouth curved into a wicked grin, showing sharp pointed teeth.

Jack's own eyes widened and the man laughed. Dark tattoos appeared on the man's tanned skin as a shimmer worked its way down his body. The woman popped off his cock and looked back at them over her shoulder. Golden cat eyes that matched her mane of golden locks looked him over. It was a visual caress to rival any he'd ever had the pleasure of getting before. He swore he heard her purr but had to be mistaken.

Lisa's throaty laugh reached his ears. "He's a demon of some sort and she's a shifter."

"A demon?" It was his first time seeing one in person. He'd dealt with a few for business but never in person.

"I'd have to get a closer look to figure out which kind.

And don't sound so shocked, Jack. You're a part of this world now. Mystics love to get out and play. We have a much more laid back view of things."

Jack focused on the woman on his lap. "Even when it comes to pubic sex?"

"Definitely when it comes to sex. For the record, this isn't exactly public. This is a safe haven to do what we want, when we want, however we want to do it. No one would bat an eye if you laid me out and ate my pussy, or if I used a strap-on to fuck your ass."

Jack wasn't too sure about the strap-on, but he was all for getting a taste of her sweet pussy again. He rocked into her again, pulling a moan from her lips. "Good to know."

Lisa's hands were at the button of his jeans in the space of a breath. They unsnapped and she rose up on her knees to unzip him. Reaching inside, she wrapped her hand around his cock and pulled it out.

Relief at having his dick out of the confines of his jeans had Jack scooting to shove the stiff material down a little, enough so the zipper wouldn't gouge into his dick. Once he situated himself, he moved Lisa away and spun her, before guiding her back between his legs.

Grabbing the base of his dick, he held it upright while guiding her back. The head breached her slick pussy lips, the heat enveloping it, tugging at his balls. She sank down and moaned.

Wrapping his arms around her, he pulled her until she leaned back against him, shuttling his dick in and out slightly.

"Is this what you wanted when we came down here?" He whispered, lips brushing against her ear.

"Yes," she panted. Her hands finding their way to her breasts where she pinched her nipples through the thin fabric of her top.

"Do you like the show next to us or the one in front?"

Lisa's head lolled to the side, toward the demon and shifter.

Jack watched as the demon pushed the shifter on all fours and mounted her from behind. A long hiss of air escaped from between the woman's lips. Her head dropped to the floor, only to be brought back up with the demon's hand fisted in her hair. The slow steady beat of flesh slapping against flesh sounded from them.

Jack felt Lisa's core flex around him. Using his arms around her, he lifted her before letting her fall back onto his cock. A small grunt came from her. "I like it," she said, voice husky, thick with arousal. He continued talking, keeping his mind off of how damn good it felt to have her impaled on him. The last thing he wanted was to come before they'd even gotten started.

"What about the one in front of us? He's shifted to human form and she's on all fours as well. If you look closely, you can see she's tied down. Knees spread. He has access to so much of her." Jack gripped her wiggling hips, attempting to keep control of the situation. She'd started bouncing quickly, the in and out slide pushing him closer to oblivion.

She looked away from the couple next to them. Breathy moans and sexy little noises escaped her lips as she continued to work her hips on him. Gasping when the centaur they were watching struck a blow with a flogger to the lower half of his woman's buttocks. White sparks shot out around the pixie, growing larger and larger with each seemingly random hit.

"He has access to whatever he wants. He can take her mouth, grab her breasts and nipples, and play with her anus and genitals. Do you want to see him ram his thick cock in her? See her sparks fly the closer she comes to orgasm?"

"Please Jack," she mewled.

He wasn't quite sure what she was asking for, but hoped to hell it was along the lines of what he wanted. He'd love to tie her up like the pixie. Love to have her submit to him. Shove his cock in her mouth then take her ass hard.

Lisa wiggled again, her body showing him she needed more. Jack gave up trying to hold her in place. He helped her bounce up and down on his dick. The tight clasping of her pussy milking him. Tingles shot up his legs and into his balls. They drew up painfully, ready to explode.

Shoving against the back of the couch, he braced himself with his back, lifting his hips up to pound into Lisa. She fell back against him, wrapping one hand around the back of his neck, the other skating down her body until she found her clit.

Turning her head she captured his lips. They ate at each other's lips. Moaning and grunting. They each gasped for breath. He knew she was close. Could feel her inner muscles rippling along his shaft. "Come on, baby. Come all over my dick."

It didn't take more than those words to have her tipping over the edge. She arched and he grabbed her hips forcing her back down. She came screaming his name and he followed behind a couple of thrusts later.

In the aftermath they sank back onto the couch. Jack wrapped his arms around her, pressing his face into her hair. He enjoyed the feel of his cock still embedded inside her. The soft fluttering of her pussy caressing him, bringing him down from the high.

A noise next to him reminded him they weren't alone. The demon stood, wearing a pair of dark cargo pants. The woman he'd been with gathered up their belongings.

"Not bad for an angel's heir," the demon drawled. "And

to snag a nymph while you're at it. Such a prized possession. If you decide you want to try something else, I'll gladly trade you for one of mine." He motioned to the female he'd been with. Her eyes flared with interest. "Ask for Valac at the bar. I have many conquests you can choose from." He spun and walked away leaving Jack stunned.

CHAPTER TWELVE

April 8th, 9:30am

"Wake up sleepy head," Lisa purred before placing a kiss on Jack's cheek. She understood his need for sleep after the previous night. After their frolic in the club basement, they went back to the main floor and danced for a couple more hours. Valac's invitation to switch partners never came up, thankfully, and they ended the night back in the room, fucking until they dropped.

Sex with him was the best it's ever been. Coming together, the melding of their bodies. Jack instinctively knew how hard or slow to take it. He pushed all of her buttons without fumbling the attempt. His confidence in playing her body like a finely tuned instrument was amazing and she was ready for more.

He'd been asleep for most of the morning, and it was time for his surprise. But in order for him to get it, he needed to wake the hell up. "Jack," she crooned next to his ear. Using her tongue, she swiped lightly across the outer shell, nipping his lobe and tugging.

Jack stretched and rolled onto his back. The sheet slid down his bare torso, the flex of muscles drew her gaze. The man was a thing of beauty, even though he'd tell her men weren't beautiful. "Hey," he grumbled sleepily, unaware of her thoughts. "Come back to bed." He reached for her and she danced away.

"Nuh, uh, uh. Get up. I have a reservation and I don't plan on missing it. Now, if you don't want to come with me and see," she shrugged casually, "then by all means, stay in bed. Alone. With nothing to do. No one to spend time with."

Jack rolled out of bed quicker than she expected, snatching her up by the waist. He hoisted her up against his hard, naked body. His erection pressing into her soft belly. "I have something to show you too." He pressed a gentle kiss on her lips before letting her slide down his body. Her nipples pebbled with the skin on skin friction.

She giggled like a smitten teenager when he let go. For the love of the Goddesses, the man was yummy. She watched his tight ass flex as he walked to the bathroom. *Beautiful*.

"How much time do I have," he called out, pulling her from her daze.

"Thirty minutes before we need to be there. Why?" She edged her way closer to the bathroom door. She knew if she got too close, she'd end up luring him into something sexual. Not that it was a bad thing. It would make them late though, and she really wanted Jack to see her in all her nymph glory. Sex could always come later. *Would* come later.

Jack poked his unruly dark head out the doorway. His eyes darkened when his gaze landed on her. It sent her girly bits tingling and a fresh wave of arousal to dampen her minuscule panties. The man had her head spinning. Had for the last few years, even though she never admitted it. Now that she'd had him, she was getting more and more attached. How would she be able to keep working for him when she felt the way she did? *This is so not a good thing*. Things would have to change. She might have to take Griff up on his offer and if that didn't work, then she'd find another job.

"Hey, are you okay?" Walking out of the bathroom still naked, he wrapped her up in his arms. She must have let her upset about the situation and switching jobs show.

Plastering a smile on her face, she hugged him back then slapped his ass playfully. "I'm fine. Get dressed so we can get going. If we're lucky, we'll have time to grab a quick bite downstairs."

Jack pressed a kiss to the top of her head. "Sure thing, babe."

While he got dressed, Lisa made a quick phone call to the concierge, changing her mind about eating with other people. She didn't want to share him with anyone else. If all she was allowing herself to have was this week with him, then she was eking out every second.

Ten minutes later they rode the elevator down to the lobby. Lisa led Jack through the lobby; passed the reception desk and the lounge they served breakfast in. Guiding him to a bank of elevators tucked discretely into the wall. Pressing her hand to the panel, the door opened silently. They rode up to the third floor and stepped out the opposite door.

"Not eating, I take it."

"I decided on something different."

Soft music played through the deserted hallway. The cool blue tones and wavy designs hinting at what lie beyond the doors they walked by. This was her favorite area of Satyr. Catering to water-bound Mystics. Cool and relaxing, it was her entire reason for coming back again and again.

Lisa got lucky and was able to reserve the biggest room on the floor. When they reached their destination, an attendant stood waiting for them. A large cart full of food was next to him; the delicious smells of bacon and pancakes wafting from beneath the silver domed lids. Her stomach rumbled but she ignored it.

The tall, lithe man waiting for them bowed deeply. "I have everything you have requested ma'am."

"Thank you." She pressed her hand on the panel to open the door. A wave of warm, salty air gusted over them as they stepped inside. Lisa breathed in the crisp, clean air as it flowed over her senses. She wanted a tropical setting for her time in the water room. Warm breezes. Rustling palms. A smooth concrete entrance led up to a pebbled walkway that went halfway around the room. There was a cabana off to the side with table and chairs. Beyond that, there was the private bathroom and shower. The focal point of the room though was the crystal clear blue water with white beach rimming it. Two towels were laid out near the water's edge waiting for them. The room was exactly as she'd desired.

Satyr went all out in order meet a client's specifications.

"Holy shit," Jack said under his breath.

"Amazing, isn't it?" She looked at him over her shoulder. The look of wonder stamped across his face was reward enough to warrant the amount of money she'd spent.

Everything in Satyr was new to him. The entire Mystic world actually. He'd had dealings with Mystics, but she doubted he'd ever walked in the Mystic life. It was a realm unlike the one he knew. Parts of the life were shrouded in such secrecy that those not involved weren't allowed to know. To a man who'd grown up in the human realm, it had to be like going to Disneyland. The Mystic realm was a magical, fantastical place where fantasies came to life.

As Jack took in the surroundings, Lisa made sure the attendant set up everything exactly as she requested. He handed her the swimsuit she'd ordered for Jack, and she passed him some money.

The elf took it and left without another word. The door closed and locked automatically behind him. He would place an *occupied* placard on the door so they wouldn't be interrupted.

"Let's have a bite to eat and talk."

Jack wandered over to the table where she stood. She handed him the swimsuit. "I thought you might want this. If not now, then to put on before we leave. I should have told you not to put on jeans."

"Thanks." He dropped down into the seat across from her, draping the shorts on the arm of the chair. "What is this place?"

Lisa plated food for them and sat. A giant heaping of bacon and eggs for him; bacon and pancakes for her. "This is a nymph sanctuary. At least right now. Each room on this floor is water themed of some sort. I snagged the biggest one for us."

A soft smile curved his mouth. "This wasn't in your plan previously?"

"No." She shoved a forkful of pancakes in her mouth to keep from saying more. She'd wanted to surprise him with something special.

She woke up early and made all of the arrangements. It helped that Paul was one of her best friends and able to secure everything so quickly. She would pay a pretty penny for it, more than her entire week at the resort, and she only had the room for a couple hours. She hoped it would be worth the exorbitant price in order to show Jack exactly who she was. To see if he liked not just the efficient woman who helped with his daily life, but the nymph as well.

The nymph didn't like scheduling meetings or typing reports. She didn't like waking up at the crack of dawn in order to get to work on time and have everything set up and ready for him. Her nymph side wanted to sleep and laze about. Nibble on snacks and find more pleasurable pursuits. She wanted sex and fun. Nightlife and dancing.

Jack devoured the eggs faster than anything he'd ever eaten. He wasn't even sure he'd tasted it but fuck if that mattered. Lisa had arranged the excursion last minute for them to share. A special surprise with him in mind. It told him he meant more than a week of fucking.

"It's fantastic. It feels like we're on a tropical island." He took a drink of orange juice and looked around again. It truly was amazing what they did in the room, and it made him curious to see what else there was.

"That was the point. Relaxing without all of the travel."

His snort came out unplanned. "I know how much you abhor that."

"Exactly!" Her plush lips wrapped around the fork as she polished off her pancakes. Damn he wanted between them again. He wanted to feel the heat of her mouth as she took his dick to the root. Her silky, smooth lips drag across his heated flesh. He'd thoroughly enjoyed it the night before.

Impulsively, he stood, kicking off his shoes and shucking his restrictive clothing. He glanced at the suit she'd handed him. It was sweet of Lisa to get it, but he wouldn't need it. Why would he want to put clothes on when he planned on taking them right off?

Whatever she had in mind bringing him here, he wanted to get down to it. He eyed her where she sat perched on her wicker chair. Her eyes roamed hungrily over him, snagging on his obvious erection. The smirk pulling at his lips couldn't be avoided. Satisfaction lit through him knowing she liked his body. Hell, he liked hers too, especially naked.

For the last three years, he'd done nothing but ogle her when she wasn't looking. Unprofessional…sure, but not as bad as hitting on her would have been the second she walked into his office that first day. He was proud of the fact he'd kept his hands to himself for as long as he did.

"Come on, babe. I want to check out the water and get your naked, wet body against mine." He held out his hand and waited for her to take it.

Slowly she rose from her seat. With the flick of her wrist, the sundress she wore dropped around her feet. She stood before him in a tiny pair of black panties, if you could even call them that. There wasn't enough material to make a coat for a mouse. He *liked* it.

Placing her hand in his, he tipped his head. "Those too."

She rolled her eyes and let go of his hand. She wiggled out of the scrap and tossed them on top of her dress. "Better?"

"Almost," he said, his voice on the husky side. Pulling her to him, he wrapped an arm around her waist and tilted her head up with his free hand. He kissed her softly, letting his mouth linger on hers. Her breathy gasp captured by his lips as he deepened the kiss. Pouring as much passion and need into it as he could. He couldn't tell her how he felt, not yet. She wasn't ready for it, but he hoped before the week was over she would be. He had one more full day to show her his love with actions.

Breaking from the kiss, he dragged her into the water. Instead of the cool water he half expected, warm liquid engulfed his feet sending shards of sensation up his legs. "Damn."

"Nice, isn't it? I like the water to be slightly warmer than they usually set it. More like a bath. I've spent enough time in chilly lake water to last a lifetime."

"Tell me about it." They waded into the middle, the water coming to his waist. Two loungers caught his eye, he left her were she stood and grabbed them. After helping her up onto one, he got on the other, holding her hand so she didn't float away. When he looked up at what should have been the ceiling, he saw clear blue skies with the occasional cloud floating by.

He didn't know how they did it. Made the room seem so normal from the outside and beyond comprehension on the inside. Whatever they did, he understood why Lisa kept coming back.

"Tell you about what? My life before coming to the company?"

"Yeah, I want to know more about you. We've worked together for three years, but I don't feel like I know anything about your personal life."

"It isn't that exciting. I'm sure it will bore you to tears."
Jack chuckled and squeezed her hand. "If it involves you, then I want to hear it."

She gusted out an irritated sigh, and he was sure she was trying to come up with a way to get out of telling him. "Fine, but don't say I didn't warn you."

He lifted her hand to his mouth and kissed the back of it. "I'm duly warned."

"My mother is a nymph and my father is a satyr. They're a randy couple and ended up having ten kids. Seven girls and three boys."

"Impressive."
Lisa snorted. "Something like that. We grew up on a big piece of land in the Lake Tahoe region of California. We're a family of water nymphs, so we like to be in or near water as much as possible."

Jack felt a frown form. "You aren't in water much. At least not that I know of."

"That's why I come here. I've gotten used to curbing my nymph side. I was sick of people seeing me as some hippy-dippy; let's have sex-all-the-time kind of girl. My sisters don't think it's a big deal. They like the stereotype. It gives them an excuse to fuck off most of the time."

"That isn't you at all." His Lisa was nothing like that. She'd worked her ass off from day one in the company. He'd checked when he decided to transfer her to his assistant.

"I know. My family doesn't understand, but then they never did. Don't get me wrong. I had my fair share of fun back in the day. It got old fast and I wanted more. There are only so many hours you can spend frolicking in the water, dancing, and playing humans for fools. People may not see being an assistant as very career-worthy, but I love it. The organization. The schedules. Managing the unmanageable. It shows a nymph can be more than a mindless sex toy."

"It sounds like you wish you weren't one."

"Oh no. I love being a nymph, especially a water one. I just like being seen as more than that. I *know* I'm more, and I get a sick sense of satisfaction proving it to my family."

"What does that mean *a water one*? I've seen you do… odd things with water, like the showering Griff got the other day." Jack chuckled remembering the look on Griff's shocked face. Jack had been too glad he hadn't been the one standing beneath the hovering mist. He was sure it would have turned into a torrential downpour if it'd been him.

A soft smile curved her mouth. "Simply put, I can manipulate water." Letting go of his hand, she dipped it in the water between them. Bringing a handful out, she put a finger from her other hand in it and twirled it. A small funnel formed into a tiny hurricane. The higher her finger, the bigger the funnel grew. With a flick, the funnel disappeared, the water going back to where it came from.

It was…"Wow. Can you only do little things like that, or do you do things on a grander scale?"

"I can do big and destructive…like send a boat off

course. My gifts tend to be more on the side of movement. My sister Amie can make water have healing properties. Dana can form springs and wetlands. We each have our specialty. When we were small, we used to make water fountains like the ones you see at water parks or concrete playgrounds. The kinds that shoot up into the air or dance to music. It's how we learn to use our inherent gifts. Figure out what we should concentrate on."

"Your life doesn't sound boring at all."

Lisa shrugged. "I guess it depends on how you look at it." She rolled off her lounger into the water. Before he could follow her into the warm depths, water shot up around him, coming down like a warm summer rain.

Rolling into the water as well, he pushed the loungers away and searched for her. His head came up and she stood before him. Lunging, he tackled her, dragging her under quickly before breaching the surface.

Her infectious giggle triggered his laughter. When his died down, he cupped her face, tilting it up. "Thank you for showing me who you really are."

He felt the heated blush beneath his palms. A flicker of shyness crossing her eyes. "I wanted you to see the other side of me. For whatever reason, the guys I've seen in the past find it fascinating for a little bit but the second I think its getting serious, they tell me they'd never choose to be with a Mystic long term. I figured that now that you're in my world, maybe you wouldn't run for the hills."

"Never! I'm not going anywhere, Lisa. I've waited too long to let this opportunity slip away."

He lowered his mouth to hers, a leisurely exploration meant to tease and seduce. She sighed, melting into him. Holy fuck, it was the best thing ever. She gave herself over to him, allowing him to drag her to the side where the towels were.

He turned, lying on his back, her straddling his hips. The softness of her pussy lips over his cock, damn near making his head explode. He couldn't wait to get inside her again.

CHAPTER THIRTEEN

April 9th, 6:00PM

Lisa opened the door to the room and was greeted by Kyron, the centaur. She'd finally remembered his name. "Hello again." She waved him and the cart he pushed through the door.

"You aren't by chance going to take me up on my offer, are you?" He asked, his deep voice rumbling from his chest.

Lisa chuckled lightly. Jack was all the man she needed. Too bad it couldn't be forever. She'd lost her head for a little while the day before in the water room. The notion they could be together after Satyr playing with her head. Jack's emergency phone call from Griffin yanked her back to reality.

It was their last night together and her heart already ached. She didn't want to say goodbye, but it became abundantly clear she would have to. She'd fallen in love with her boss. It hadn't happened over night or during the last couple days. It happened gradually over the last three years. These few days with him only made her realize how head-over-heels in love she was. "Sorry, but no. I'm quite happy with the man I'm with."

Kyron's rueful smile tugged at his lips. "His good fortune will forever be my loss. Would you like this laid out on the table?"

"Please." She swept by him to finish lighting the candles. Jack would be back soon and she wanted everything ready. There would be no interruptions after his return. The front desk knew to hold all calls or allow room services to come by. She planned to steal his phone away and hide it from him until morning.

The soft clanking of dishes and silverware echoed through the room. When it stopped, she turned to see Kyron observing her. "This man you are with, you're in love with him?"

A blush stole across her cheeks, radiating heat. "What makes you say that?" It wasn't that she was embarrassed about loving him. It was that it was so easy for a stranger to tell; yet the man himself couldn't figure it out.

"It is the only reason I can think of for a nymph to refuse the invitations of so many. It hasn't gone unnoticed that you are here. Nymphs are prized in the club, and you could have your choice of any man or woman. Yet, you did not take Valac up on his offer. The man who brought you dinner the other night said you barely acknowledged him. And you have refused me twice. Rumor has it you even reserved the Tropical room for a liaison and that doesn't come cheep. Mystics do not waste coin on something so extravagant on someone who is only a fling."

"But that's all it is — a fling." *It can't be more.* "After tomorrow I'll be free."

The sound of the door slamming had her squeezing her eyes tight. Damn, she hoped Jack hadn't heard the last part. Or maybe it was for the best that he had. It would make tomorrow easier on her when she was forced to cut ties. The thought made her heart clench and pain radiate through it.

Jack rounded the corner, hot anger blazing in his eyes. Her stomach dropped. He'd heard what she said. She could tell by the look on his face.

Kyron looked between them and dipped his head. "If you'll excuse me, I have to get back to work."

Lisa moved toward him, his tip in her hand.

He lifted his own to stop her. "Thank you, but you have been generous enough." He left, pulling the empty cart behind him.

The look of anger faded from Jack's face. "You did say only for this week. Let's sit down and eat. I'd hate to waste the delicious meal you've ordered."

Lisa took a seat at the small table and waited for him to join her. He shook his head, frown marring his handsome face. Unfortunately, she didn't feel like eating anymore. The food was dry and wooden in her mouth; she was barely able to choke it down.

This was her last moment with the man she'd fallen in love with; she could feel it. Her last moment to take in the beauty of his features in the candlelight before she said goodbye forever. Her last moment to bask in the warmth of his embrace, though she doubted that would be happening now. Not with the look of anger and betrayal on his face.

Yes, she'd made the right decision. She couldn't take Griff up on his offer no matter how appealing it was. She would be putting in her two-week notice first thing Monday morning. After spending the weekend grieving for the job she loved and the man who'd stolen her heart.

She watched Jack visibly shut down. His eyes turned cold and emotionless. He looked away, sipping the red wine she'd picked with him in mind. It came from one of the wineries close to where she was from. Paul kept a couple bottles on hand for her. In the back of her mind, she thought to share more of her life with him.

It'd been silly and foolish, and evidently wrong.

CHAPTER FOURTEEN

April 10th, 10:00am

Lisa rolled over in bed and flailed. She squeezed her eyes shut in an attempt to keep the pain at bay. Too quickly she'd gotten used to Jack's warm, strong body next to her. Yet, he wasn't there now. His side of the bed was cold. His pillow never slept on.

"Oh my god," she breathed harshly. "I miss him." Tears burned the backs of her eyes, and her breath clogged in her lungs.

Flopping onto her back, she replayed the events of the night before.

Dinner with Jack had been heartbreaking, and she wasn't sure she'd ever recover from it. When he calmly pushed his plate of partially eaten food away and stood, she knew he wasn't staying.

He packed his bag quietly with his few belongings, as she dumbly looked on. It took him less than five minutes and before she knew it, he stood before her, staring down with sad eyes.

He kissed her. Softly. Reverently. Like a man who knew he would never do it again. She didn't have time to react. To grab him and hold him tightly against her body.

Without a word he left. He just turned and walked away without a backwards glance.

They didn't talk about her fling statement. They didn't talk about what would happen next.

He took what she'd said their first night together as gospel, never knowing she would have gladly changed her mind. With one word, one hint, she would have told him how she felt if it meant he'd still be with her now.

Groaning, Lisa shucked the covers from her body and climbed out of bed. There was no sense in staying any later, dragging out her last few hours in a place that now reminded her of him. It would be best to pack her belongings and head back to her apartment. Start the grieving process and write her resignation. Maybe she would email it to him over the weekend.

She was such a coward.

CHAPTER FIFTEEN

April 13th, 8:00am

THE OFFICES OF MORGAN & POWERS DESIGN AND
ARCHITECTURE

Lisa walked into work Monday morning with a ball of
trepidation knotting her stomach. As soon as she'd gotten
to her apartment on Friday, she'd written and fired off her
resignation, afraid she wouldn't have the nerve to do it later.
She knew Jack read it. She had the *read receipt* sitting in her
email. He never responded though.

No email.

No phone call.

No dropping in unannounced, pounding on her door
demanding to know what the hell she was thinking.

Okay, so the last wouldn't have happened anyway.
She wasn't sure he even knew where she lived, and she'd
been fairly straightforward in the email as to why she was
quitting.

She couldn't continue working for him after their week
together. There was no way they could go back to how it was

before she'd gotten a taste of him. Before she'd showed him a part of her no one saw.

Saturday she'd cried like she'd never cried before, and then called her mother for comfort. Her loony family may not understand her need to be different, but they were there for her when she was down. Her mother bought her a plane ticket to come home ten minutes after they got off the phone. Lisa was scheduled to leave after finishing her last day of work and head straight to the airport.

Putting her purse in the bottom drawer of her desk, she took her overcoat off and hung it up. Jack wasn't in yet, so she decided to act as though it was any other day.

She put a pot of coffee on and checked emails while she waited. Midway through the backlog, the door to her office opened and in walked Jack.

She steeled her spine and plastered a professional smile on her face. Her hungry gaze roamed over his handsome frame. He wore a dark gray suit that hugged his wide shoulders. It looked stunning against his tan face and dark unruly hair. Her breath caught in her throat, and her heart beat out of control when he turned to the person next to him. Lisa hadn't even noticed he wasn't alone. Jack and the unknown person were talking in hushed tones. It looked intimate and personal. Jealousy reared its head and tried to grab hold.

Jack tipped his head back suddenly and laughed at something his companion said. He stepped to the side and motioned the person forward.

A petite blonde woman in a tight little outfit and black fuck-me heels stepped in front of him. She laughed demurely and fluttered her eyes at him.

Jack put his hand on her lower back and escorted her farther into the office. Lisa was so stunned by his demeanor toward the other woman that it took her a moment to realize they'd stopped in front of her desk.

"Lisa," Jack barked harshly, snagging her attention.

Lisa shot to her feet, pad of paper and pencil in hand by automatic reflex. "Yes, Mr. Morgan."

His jaw clenched and his nostrils flared. "Put those down. Grab your stuff and head home. Pamela is taking over your job as of right now. We'll consider your two-week notice as two weeks paid vacation. You do have plenty of unused time saved up and, like you told me, you never get any time off to be alone."

Lisa's mouth dropped open. She snapped it shut when the blonde smirked. "It's fine Mr. Morgan. I'll work my two weeks."

He wasn't even listening. He turned away and headed into his office. "No, I insist. It's been a pleasure working with you." The door shut behind him and she still wasn't sure what the hell had just happened.

Lisa turned to her replacement. The woman's smooth grin rocked the corners of her mouth. A smarmy little look on her face. "I'll get you up to speed," Lisa said dully.

"No thanks. I've been eyeing this job for a *long* time. I know exactly what to do to *please* the boss. Now, if you could get your stuff and leave, I'd appreciate it. Jack and I have work to do."

Mind numb and not knowing what else to do, Lisa grabbed her purse and her coat then left. There wasn't anything else for her to take home. She didn't have personal items in the desk, preferring to keep the two sides separate. If only she'd stuck to the oath she'd put in place so long ago.

"Toodle-oo," Pamela called out. "Bitch." The low words managed to reach Lisa's ear. She spun to say something when Jack's voice came through the secretary's speaker.

"Pamela, could I get you to come in here please? I need your help with a couple of things."

"Of course, Jack," Pamela purred back. She sashayed to the door, disappearing behind the wood.

Before Lisa could turn away from the sight, Griff walked in. Lisa looked at him and tears welled in her eyes. This wasn't how it was supposed to be. She wasn't supposed to hurt so damn bad at being replaced. She bolted through the door and raced to her car as fast as she could.

Griff watched Lisa run to the elevator. Tears had been shimmering in her dark eyes. He was torn between chasing her down to comfort her and finding his partner to see what the hell he'd done to scare her away.

Heading into Jack's office won out. They had a meeting set up in an hour, and they needed to go over a few things. Business had to take precedence.

Strolling into the other room, Griff was greeted by the sight of a small, tight ass leaning over Jack's desk. Toned, bare legs led to black fuck-me heels, and Griff's dick was instantly hard. He adjusted himself before clearing his throat.

"Hey Jack, where was Lisa off to? I thought we had a meeting in a bit."

Jack looked up, hurt and anger burning in his eyes.

Fuck. The week must not have gone over well. He knew something like that would happen. Lisa was a great woman, but he didn't think she was worth throwing away their professional relationship.

The hot chick leaning over Jack's desk straightened and turned around. She batted her baby blue eyes at him and puckered her lips in a practiced move. She leaned toward him, and he couldn't help his gaze trailing down to her cleavage, which was on display. "Oh hi," she said breathless. "I'm Pamela. You must be Griff." She held her hand out, but he got the impression he was supposed to kiss it, not shake it. His erection died an instant death. He did not do prima donnas. "It's Mr. Powers," he said tightly. "Leave. I need to talk to my partner."

The blonde stuck her lower lip out and pouted. She dropped her hand and looked back over at Jack. "Jack?" She questioned.

Griff didn't think Jack would save her and he was right. "Go on out, Pamela. I'll buzz you when we're ready."

Pamela sucked in a big breath, thrusting her chest out. "If you say so, Jack."

It took everything in Griff's power not to throw the woman out. She sauntered past him and threw a sultry look at him over her shoulder as she walked out the door.

Griff slammed it behind her.

"What the fuck did you do?" He yelled, unable to rein in his own anger. If Jack had hired that woman to make Lisa jealous, then it was a shit move.

Jack leaned back in his chair, arms crossed over his chest, seemingly unbothered by what happened. "I don't know what you're talking about. I got a new assistant when my other one turned in her resignation on Friday."

"What!"

"Lisa quit. I needed an assistant. I'm not sure what you aren't understanding about the situation."

"You fucking moron."

Jack glared at Griff, and Griff glared right back.

"She didn't give a two-week notice?"

"She did. I decided not to bother with it."

"So, you brought that bimbo in here, flaunting her in front of Lisa, to what, make her feel like shit. Did you send Lisa packing too?"

Jack's jaw clenched and popped. "Yep."

"You're an asshole. What the fuck happened last week? What did you do?"

Jack shot up out of his chair. Fucking Griff acting like it was Jack's fault. "I didn't do shit. She said it was a fling. One week only."

"And you wanted more."

"Yes, but apparently she didn't."

"Did you tell her how you feel?"

"No, I thought she'd get the hint. I showed her in every possible way that I wanted more. I thought she'd be the one to bring up changing the rules she set down. It was our last night together and she never brought it up."

Griff pulled out the chair and dropped into it. "Holy shit, you're dumb. When have you ever known a woman to take a hint?"

Griff had him there, but he'd never tell him. "Fuck you."

"No, dude. Fuck you. She left here in tears. You could see on her face that she was hurt."

Jack's entire body tensed. The thought of her in tears because of him tore at his heart. He refused to believe it was because of him. He heard her making plans to hook up with another man. "She was probably upset I replaced her so quick. There was no fucking way I could stand two weeks of being around her and not having her in my life like I want."

"You make my head hurt. You love her but you won't

tell her or fight for her. Maybe you aren't as into her as you thought you were. I mean, if I'd found the one person who made life worth living, I'd move heaven and earth to be with her. Hell, I'd even take a kick to the balls if it meant she'd be back in my arms."

Jack sat back down, rolling up to his desk, resting forearms on it. "What the hell do you care? You didn't want me to see her in the first place."

"I didn't because I thought something like this would happen."

"No, you thought she'd try to take me for a ride. Demand more money or promote her somehow."

"Fine. Yeah, in the back of my mind I'm clinging to that bullshit with Felicity, but I never actually believed Lisa would do the same thing. I wanted you to be careful and lay your cards out on the table, not play mind games with the woman. What did she say in her resignation?"

"It would be too hard to go back to how things were. She couldn't be *just* my assistant anymore."

"That's good though, right? All of this can be fixed with a simple conversation. Or is there something else?"

Jack couldn't look his friend in the eyes. He stared off into the distance as her words played through his head again. "After helping you out over the phone, I got back and overheard her telling this guy who'd been hitting on her since day one, *but that's all it is – a fling. I'll be free after tomorrow.* It pissed me off when I heard her say that to a complete stranger. I thought we were moving in the right direction. We had a couple of amazing days together and a nice candlelit dinner planned. I was going to tell her what's been in my heart for what feels like forever. And holy shit, I sound like a girl."

Griff chuckled, not bothering to cover it up. "You sound like a man in love. What happened?"

"We had dinner. We never talked about what I'd heard. She knows I did too. After eating, I packed my shit and left. I don't know what she did after that. Friday I got her resignation via email."

"And you were still butt hurt about her *fling* statement that you thought you'd hurt her by bringing the bimbette in? I have to tell ya, I'm not impressed, and I'm not sure you're the same guy I've known most of my life. I've never known you to give up so easily on something. You do still want her, don't you?"

"Yes," Jack grunted. With every fiber in his body, he wanted her. The weekend had been miserable without her next to him. He'd tossed and turned; questioning everything he did, wondering if he should have done things differently. Wondering if he should call or show up on her doorstep. He thought he'd give her time to miss him, and arrogantly, he'd thought she would make the first move. When she didn't, he got pissed all over again and hired the first girl he'd come across in the personnel files. Which was proving to be an epic mistake judging by Griff's reaction to the woman. The man loved women and she'd instantly turned him into an asshole.

"If you ask me, I think you're scared. You've never had to work to get a woman's affections. It seems they always come out and tell you they love you within two minutes of meeting you. Lisa didn't and now you're afraid to make the next move. Grow a set, man."

The conversation was cut short when Pamela buzzed in. Jack noticed the time and knew they'd have to get to work. He had a lot to think about. There might be some validity in Griff's words.

CHAPTER SIXTEEN

April 27th, 8:00am

LISA'S APARTMENT

Lisa pulled the covers over her head, hoping the person at her door would go away. She'd flown in late the previous night and definitely hadn't gotten enough sleep.

Pounding on the door resumed and she groaned, rolling over and shoving her head deeper under the covers. Why wouldn't whoever it was go away? Grumbling, she pulled her tired ass out of bed, not caring what she looked like. A quick pat down of her body as she stumbled to the door confirmed she, at least, had clothes on. "Good enough."

She blindly unlocked the door, cracking her eyes open finally when she turned the knob. "Do you have any idea what time it is?" she croaked, attempting to get her eyes to focus.

"Yes," a deep voice rumbled, shocking her enough to clear the fuzziness from her brain. Strong arms scooped her up. A door slammed and before she could say boo, and she was being carried into the living room. "What the hell are you doing answering the door dressed like that?"

Jack's voice tripped down her spine, flowing over her like a cool rush of water. Just hearing it thrust her back to the week they spent together. Made her long do to it all over again.

She couldn't get her brain to function enough to answer, so she nuzzled her face into the side of his neck. His warm skin and intoxicating scent played havoc on her body. Her nipples perked beneath the soft cotton of her shirt. Her pussy spasmed in want. She'd missed him the two weeks she'd been in California. No amount of consoling or cavorting in the lake could heal her shattered heart. Eventually, she gave up trying and flew home amidst her parents' protests.

Jack's arms tightened around her like bands of steel. He settled them on the couch and pressed a kiss to her forehead. "Damn, I've missed you, babe. Where've you been? I've been trying to get hold of you for over a week."

Lisa wasn't in a state of mind where she could resist him. Not now, after weeks of sleepless nights and one longer-than-it-probably-was flight back to Denver. "I went home after you kicked me out."

Jack moved her away slightly and cupped her face. "I'm sorry I did that. I was an ass. I was hurt and didn't know how to deal with it. I thought you would figure out I was in love with you without me having to tell you. When I overheard you telling that guy it was only a fling, I overreacted."

"You're in love with me?"

Jack snorted. Damn, he'd been so stupid. For too long he'd held onto the belief that she should be the one to say *I love you* first. That she would instinctively know how he felt. As much as he'd like to blame his idiocy on the fact she knew everything else he was thinking before he did, he couldn't. It was something that needed to come from him. And now that he'd said it, it suddenly dawned on him how easy it had been. "Yeah. I thought you knew." He kissed her softly on the lips, and then let go of her face.

She blinked rapidly. "I...I didn't," she said licking her lips. "I didn't know what to think. You agreed so quickly to the *week only* idea, I assumed that was all you wanted. That all of the time we've spent together over the years made you wonder what it would be like to sleep with me, and my time off was the perfect chance since you knew no one from work would see us."

"Absolutely not. Come on, Lisa. You know me. I don't play around with employees, and I definitely wouldn't mess with the best damn assistant I've ever had unless I wanted to take our relationship to the next level. We're perfect together. You make every day easier just by being there."

Her eyes narrowed suspiciously. "And you've been without me for two-weeks, and this is the first time I've heard from you. Did something happen at the company while I was away that made you realize you need me? Did that slut Pamela do something to screw my perfect schedule up?"

"Nothing happened that Janet couldn't handle. And I've been trying to get hold of you for a while. Ask your neighbors."

"What about calling or emailing me? I do have access to both."

"You wouldn't have answered. I've messed up enough times at work to know better. I hurt you, and the only way you'd be able to tell I was sincere was if I was right in front of you—face to face."

Lisa had the good grace to look away sheepishly. "Maybe."

He turned her head back with a finger to her cheek. He wanted her to see the truth of the words reflected in his eyes. "Do you believe me then? I love you, Lisa. I need you in my life."

117

"Not just professionally? I *am* a fantastic assistant."

"Yes, professionally, but always personally. I want you to be my partner in all aspects of my life."

"Well, I forgive you for being an ass. All you needed to do was talk to me that night you left Satyr."

"You could have talked to me too."

"I know, but I didn't know how to tell you I wanted more. I didn't want to ruin what we had with what I wanted."

"And what is it you wanted?"

"More time with you to see where this might go."

"It's going all the way."

A smile curved her lips and Jack didn't resist capturing them with his. Tongues slid against each other lazily. Both of them tasting and nipping. When he pulled back, Lisa was panting. Her eyes glazed with arousal.

"Is there something you want to tell me?" He asked, his voice lower than normal.

Her brows puckered and eyes cleared. "You think it's that easy?"

"Shouldn't it be?" A half grin inched up one side of his mouth.

Lisa rolled her eyes and grinned. "I love you too, Jack."

"Good," he grunted and peeled her shirt off.

She slapped her hands over her breasts. "Hey, what are you doing?"

"I thought we could seal our love by making love."

"Of course you did," she giggled and wiggled off his lap. The sight of her on her knees between his legs would forever be branded in his mind. Just like her declaration of love.

EPILOGUE

April 30th

Chloe waited impatiently in her chambers for Gabriel to make his appearance. She'd summoned him over an hour ago, and he'd yet to arrive. She was dressed and desperate to pop back to the human realm. She needed to verify the couple she'd matched were *in* love and not wavering in their commitment. Gabriel was her insurance in case they weren't. She doubted he would have a problem dragging the man, Jack, away if a little persuasion was needed.

Losing this early in the bet with Eros was not an option. Not after the first three months had gone by with relative ease.

A thunder-like crack sounded in the room seconds before Gabriel finally appeared. "I'm here as you demanded, Chloe. Does this mean you're ready to toss that boy you're playing with aside for me?"

Chloe snorted and grabbed him by the wrist. "No, not at this time. I have another use for you." Without further comment, she whisked them directly into the couple's bedroom. A surprised squeak came from the tiny woman whose legs were wrapped around the man's waist. He had her pushed up against the wall, fucking her. His taut ass flexed with each thrust. It was a glorious sight to behold and made her think of Eros. She could imagine him taking her the same way.

"At least someone is getting laid," Chloe said approaching them.

"Jack," the woman hissed, but he was already sliding her down the wall and shoving her behind him.

"Have a little decency," Gabriel said, tossing the blanket he'd snatched from somewhere at the couple.

Jack wrapped it around his waist and scowled. "What are you two doing here?"

"Are you in love?" Chloe asked. She wanted confirmation to calm her nerves, not confrontation.

"What does it matter to you?" Lisa asked, stepping around Jack.

"Damn it," Jack grumbled, stretching the blanket out in front of her.

"Oh please," Lisa batted his efforts away. "I'm not bothered about showing some skin. It is the nymph way."

"Goddess, I love the sight of a nymph," Gabriel said, drawing everyone's attention. His mouth curved into a wicked smile and lust rolled off him.

"Well, they don't need to see it. You're all mine. It's the *Jack* way." He pulled at the woman's arm, tugging her in front of him. Jack wrapped the blanket around her front, covering them both.

"Is it not enough that he is one of yours, Gabriel? Must you try to lure his woman away as well?"

"What?" the tiny woman exclaimed, her gaze bouncing from Gabriel to Jack to Gabriel again.

"These are the two who showed up in my office and made me who I am. They're the reason I was able to claim you at Satyr."

Chloe pursed her lips and assessed the couple in front of her as they talked. The man was possessive of his woman and she didn't protest. Lust filled the air along with the heavy scent of sex.

"Answer my question, Jack," Chloe barked. "Are you in love with this nymph? Is she the one you choose to be with for the rest of your life, or should I have Gabriel take you back to our realm to join his forces? You would gain wings and near immortality. The ability to walk between realms and drink the ambrosia from Zeus's well."

"Yes, we're in love. I have always wanted to spend the rest of my days with Lisa," Jack answered.

"And my offer holds no appeal to you?"

"No."

"Then what took you so long? I gave you plenty of time to fall in love. Why did it take you until a couple of days ago to profess how you felt?" If Chloe could figure out why the human acted so irrationally, then she hoped to avoid it the next time.

Lisa laughed, the husky sound echoing through the room. "Because he is a man, and men think woman should be the ones to say *it* first. It strokes their egos even if they do not feel the same. Luckily for him, I've loved him for years. Forgiving his idiocy wasn't a hardship."

"I'll take that into consideration next time. Humans are such strange creatures. Come Gabriel. I do believe they would like to finish fucking." Chloe had everything she needed to show Eros the couple was in love. Their

122

confession was recorded into the sands of time. He would be able to see she'd done the job.

With a flick of her wrist, she and Gabriel vanished, appearing in her chambers once again.

"You didn't need me for that Chloe," he said.

"You were insurance. A threat in case they didn't confess their love for one another."

Gabriel grunted. "I think there is more to it than that. But I can already tell you won't admit it. Next time you summon me, I hope it's for something more pleasurable." He bowed and disappeared. There was no thunder-like crack as he left. Only a warm breeze that caressed her body from her head to her toes. She would have to keep Gabriel in mind for when she was done with Eros.

THE END

Thane: January
Mystic Zodiac, Book 1

Fallen Angel Thane has been exiled to the realm of humans
and Mystics for almost fifty years after what he considers a
slight misunderstanding, too bad Zeus didn't agree. After
the blush of exile wears off, Thane dedicates his new life
to helping those in need, all in the hope of impressing the
imposing God.

A visit from his Watcher with one more task sets Thane
up to finally get what he's dreamed about for decades…
his rightful place back on Olympus with his brothers. All
he needs to do is keep one woman from "doing something
stupid." He determined to ignore his body responding for
the first time in almost fifty years in order to go home.

Amara Hope is desperate to bring her brother home,
traveling into the heart of Viral City day after day putting
her life at risk. As her last living relative, he's all she has left.
When a hunky Good Samaritan grudgingly offers help, she's
all too willing to accept. Once they get her brother home and
begin spending more time together, the more Amara knows
he's the one for her.

What the two don't know is that the Gods are playing games
with their lives, and they're on a collision course with love.

Word Count: 32,299

Genre: Paranoraml Romance
Featuring Angel

Parvati: February
Mystic Zodiac, Book 2

Parvati Shiva, a true descendent of the Goddess of love and devotion, is fed up. She runs a successful dating site, connecting Mystics and humans all over the world with their one true love. The only she hasn't been able to find love for is…her.

When a hacker gets into her network and website, shutting down her site in the height of the busy season, she calls on her cousin Jag for help, who in turn reaches out to an old friend.

Colin Patterson, IT guru and confirmed bachelor, quickly agrees to help his friend's sister out with her computer problem, hoping it will be a long drawn out process. He's eager to escape his mother's matchmaking Valentine's Day party. She's invited all of the single women — and a few men — to jump-start his dating life, something he has no interest in at all.

One mistaken identity later, Colin ruins his chance with the beautiful Indian woman he's instantly attracted to. Will he be able to prove he isn't a boss bashing idiot, save Parvati's company, and win her affections before he doesn't have a reason to stick around?

Warning: This book contains a geeky hero who can't keep his mouth shut, a strong willed businesswoman dealing in love, and an attraction that neither can deny.

Please note: This book has a hot M/M scene.

Word Count: 26,817
Genre: Paranoraml Romance
Featuring Goddess

Gideon: March
Mystic Zodiac, Book 3

Gideon Deckard is finally getting a little time away from the Keystone Predator Pack to go wolf. All he has planned is a week of running wild through the Grand Canyon before the hiking season starts back up. Once it does, he'll go back to what he does best...being the Alpha he was born to be.

Ryder Sparks can barely contain her excitement. She's taking a week off from work at the family store, Sparks Sporting & Outdoors, and going on her dream vacation. A four-day hiking trip on a lesser traveled trek through the Grand Canyon. The season has opened early and she was the first to get the coveted pass. She's looking forward to pushing herself on her first solo trip and discovering who she was really meant to be.

A run in with a massive grey wolf has Ryder stumbling and getting knocked out. When she wakes up, she's back in her tent and there's a hunky man there to help her get back on her feet. When she finds out he's a wolf-shifter instead of freaking out, she decides to go on the adventure of a lifetime with him. Now all she has to do is convince Gideon to give her a chance to be his one and only Luna.

Word Count: 36,270

Genre: Paranoraml Romance, Shifters
Featuring Wolf Shifter

About the Author

Brandy is a paranormal romance author who, on occasion, likes to dabble with contemporary. She's addicted to MDK shows and who-done-its. You'll almost never see her without some type of skull paraphernalia on and is always dreaming of more tattoos.

Brandy is a Navy brat, prior enlisted Army, current Army wife, and mom. She lives in Virginia with her husband of almost 20 years, their three kids and one dog.

Brandy is all over the web. Pick one or all to keep up with her.
Don't forget to sign up for the newsletter. There is a monthly giveaway and when the mood strikes other fun things like deep discounts in the shop.

Website | Facebook Author | Twitter | Pinterest | Tsu | Tumblr | Ello

Get Your Shop On
Newletter

Or email her at: brandy@brandywalker.net

Craving More
Tiger Nip, Book 1

TEZ Publishing

Corrine Hart is ready for few days off for rest and relaxation. At the top of her to-do list is spending as much time as possible in tiger form and doing her best to banish all thoughts of the mysterious Hunky Cupcake Guy who spent the last two weeks driving her libido insane.

Jett Montgomery-Murphy just wants to know if the tasty treats that keep showing up at work are the same ones his best friend used to get while they were in college. A trip out to Sweet Confections confirms what he thought and brings him in close contact with the one woman he's secretly lusted after for years, his best friend's sister Corrine.

A late night tryst leads to two tigers finding their mates and two humans unsure what to do next. Add in an overbearing brother, a best friend with her own drama, and a crazy ex-girlfriend that has a checkered past and you have a recipe for disaster.

Will Corrine and Jett be able to overcome the unexpected obstacles on their way to falling in love? Or will they throw in the towel before the relationship even gets off the ground?

~~~~~

Genre: Paranoraml Romance, Shifters
Featuring Tiger Shifter

Claiming More
Tiger Nip, Book 2

TEZ Publishing

Sampson Hart has known Mary Jane Poppy for ten years. She's his sister's best friend, business partner, and has had a crush on Sam for years. When the mating pull hits him, he's ready to claim her as his own. Given their history, it should be simple. Right?

MJ has loved Sam since she was fifteen. But being a hybrid, she's been told all her life she won't have a mate. When Sam proclaims she belongs to him, she doesn't believe it; the mating pull isn't there, and Sam isn't meant to be hers.

Running back home to escape the love she feels for Sam, MJ agrees to become the companion of a man who lost his mate and has three young children to raise. It is the only way to set Sam free to find the one he is truly meant to be with.

Will Sam be Claiming More or will the one he desires the most find comfort in the arms of another?

~~~~~

Genre: Paranoraml Romance, Shifters
Featuring Tiger Shifter

Dallas & Kacie: Tiger Bite
Tiger Nip, Book 2.5

TEZ Publishing

It's the holiday season and Kacie Cook is counting down the hours until its time to close up Sweet Confections. Not that she has any great plans for the week the bakery is closed. She won't be seeing her family — yet again, and all of her friends are too busy. All she has planned is a little rest and relaxation. That is until the last customer of the night walks in. Could he be the one to bring some holiday cheer and possibly change her life forever?

~~~~~

Genre: Paranoraml Romance, Shifters
Featuring Tiger Shifter

Other Books by Brandy Walker
TEZ PUBLISHING

Tiger Nip
Craving More, Book 1
Claiming More, Book 2
Dallas & Kacie: Tiger Bite, Book 2.5
Finding More, Book 3 (future release)
Giving More, Book 4 (future release)
Seeing More, Book 5 (future release)

Freefall
Caught in the Moment, Book 1
Fly Guy Next Door, Book 2
Captured by Color, Book 3 (future release)
Revving Her Engine, Book 4 (future release)
Spinning Out of Control, Book 5 (future release

Mystic Zodiac
Thane | January | Angel, Book 1
Parvati | February | God/Goddess, Book 2
Gideon | March | Shifter, Book 3
Lisa | April | Nymph, Book 4
Celeste | May | Fae (releasing May 2015)
Willow | June | Witch/Warlock (releasing Jun 2015)
Amber | July | Siren (releasing Jul 2015)
Adrian | August | Dragon (releasing Aug 2015)
Colby | September | Djinn (releasing Sep 2015)
Lucas | October | Vampire (releasing Oct 2015)
Mace | November | Spirit (releasing Nov 2015)
Falcon | December | Demon (releasing Dec 2015)

Praetorian Guards
New series in the works

Keystone Predators
Under Her Spell, Book 1 (June 2015)

DECADENT PUBLISHING

ROAR LINE

Shifter U
Shifted Plans Book 1
Changing Her Tune, Book 2 (future release)

www.ingramcontent.com/pod-product-compliance
Lightning Source LLC
Chambersburg PA
CBHW030233180626
46810CB00008B/3111